She couldn't ignore his eyes.

Maybe this arrangement wasn't such a good idea after all. "You know, babysitting wasn't part of our agreement."

"I've got to do something to pay you back for that lemon pie you made." One side of his mouth tilted up. "Besides, I like spending time with the twins."

A burst of childish laughter came from the yard, and Emily saw the echo of her own smile on Abel's face. Her heart bobbed and dipped crazily and her cheeks started to burn.

She'd never had anybody to share such parenting moments with, and there was an intimacy that unsettled her, making her feel like her most vulnerable spots were unprotected.

Abel's smile suddenly faded. "I think you'd better get going." There was a strange tone in his voice and a stunned intensity in his eyes that struck her like an electric shock.

This was bad. Those silly little sparks flashing between them weren't one-sided. Abel was feeling them, too, and that could only mean one thing.

Trouble.

Laurel Blount lives on a small farm in middle Georgia with her husband, David, their four children, a milk cow, dairy goats, assorted chickens, an enormous dog, three spoiled cats and one extremely bossy goose with boundary issues. She divides her time between farm chores, homeschooling and writing, and she's happiest with a cup of steaming tea at her elbow and a good book in her hand.

Books by Laurel Blount

Love Inspired

A Family for the Farmer

A Family
for the Farmer

Laurel Blount

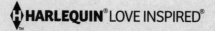

LOVE INSPIRED BOOKS

Recycling programs for this product may not exist in your area.

ISBN-13: 978-0-373-71986-0

A Family for the Farmer

Copyright © 2016 by Laurel Blount

www.Harlequin.com

Printed in U.S.A.

Make it your ambition to lead a quiet life, to mind your own business, and to work with your hands, just as we told you.
                                    —*1 Thessalonians* 4:11

In memory of my mother,
Frances Russell Medcalf,
who encouraged me to dream,
and for my husband, David,
who made all those crazy dreams come true.

Chapter One

"I don't want a peanut butter sandwich. I want one of the hamburgers we smelled outside." Five-year-old Phoebe's voice sounded unusually whiny, and Emily Elliott sighed as she dropped the baggie-wrapped offering back into her purse.

She knew her children were tired. She'd had to roust them out of bed early to make the drive down to Pine Valley from Atlanta in time for this appointment with her grandmother's lawyer. She could have saved herself all that heroic rushing around, because the attorney had already kept them waiting twenty minutes.

And of course his office *would* have to be located downwind of the small town's one and only fast food restaurant.

"You can't have a hamburger, Pheebs. There's no money." Paul spoke calmly to his twin as he flipped through the book on reptiles he'd just pulled out of his backpack. "There never is."

Emily's heart clenched, and she cast a quick glance over to the desk where the sleek secretary was busily clicking the keys on her computer. The other woman caught her eye and gave Emily a pitying smile. She'd heard.

Emily felt her face flush. It didn't matter, she reminded herself sternly. She was here to get the details of her grandmother's estate settled, not to impress Jim Monroe's secretary.

Her daughter pushed her bottom lip out. "I'm tired of sitting here. You said this would take just a few minutes, but we've been waiting a really long time."

"We *have* been waiting a long time." Emily shifted uneasily in her chair. She really hoped Mr. Monroe wasn't going to ask her to reschedule this meeting. If she had to drive down again, it would cost gas money she didn't have, and she'd have to ask Mr. Alvarez for another day off.

Asking for this one off had been bad enough.

Well, there was no point fretting over all that now. "All things work for good for those who love the Lord and are called according to His purpose," her minister had assured the congregation last Sunday. Surely that included late lawyers and cranky bosses. Emily forced a smile and smoothed a stray tendril of blond hair away from her daughter's sulky face. "Try to be patient, honey. I don't think it'll be much longer."

"Here, Pheebs." Her son pushed his reptile book over so that it rested halfway in his sister's lap. "You can share my book. It shows the inside of the lizards, not just the outsides. See? That's his guts."

"Eeww!" Phoebe made a face, but soon she was as absorbed in the book as her brother.

Emily sighed again and fished the rejected sandwich out of her bag. She was starving, and those hamburgers *had* smelled good. She broke off a small chunk and tucked it discreetly in her mouth while avoiding looking in the direction of the elegant secretary. The peanut butter stuck to the roof of her mouth and made her long for the travel thermos of double-strength coffee she'd left in the cup holder of her elderly compact car.

The twins were almost to the end of the lizard book. By the vigorous way Phoebe was kicking her small tennis shoes against the legs of her chair, Emily knew that keeping her small daughter appropriately behaved was about to get even harder. Something had to give.

Emily rose, and the twins looked up at her expectantly. "I'm going to walk outside and let the children stretch their legs for a minute. We'll be right back."

The secretary glanced away from her computer screen and blinked. "Of course," she murmured politely. "Why don't you give me your cell phone number in case Mr. Monroe comes in while you're out?"

"Mama doesn't give out her cell phone number," Paul interjected helpfully. "It's just for emergencies. Minutes cost money. Like hamburgers."

The secretary's gaze slid over to her son, and Emily was suddenly aware of how rumpled and sticky they all looked after the three-hour drive in her old car with its wonky air-conditioning system. She tilted up her chin.

"We'll come back in about fifteen minutes. I'm sure Mr. Monroe won't mind waiting for us if he gets back before then." The secretary looked as if she thought Mr. Monroe probably *would* mind, but Emily was past caring. She pushed open the heavy door and ushered the twins out into the early-summer sunshine.

It was only eleven thirty in the morning, but the Georgia heat had already settled over the town like a hot, moist blanket. Emily hesitated in front of the old storefront that housed the lawyer's office, blinking in the strong sunlight.

Jim Monroe's office faced the town square. The brick courthouse loomed directly across the street from where they stood. Its lawn looked lushly green, and shade from a huge magnolia tree dappled a bench near a concrete war memorial. Emily took her twins' hands and headed in that direction, hoping to put some distance between Phoebe and the smell of grilling burgers.

While the twins ran off some of their energy chasing each other around the tree's gnarled trunk, Emily sat on the bench nibbling at the sticky sandwich and feeling uncomfortably conspicuous. Passersby curiously glanced her way, and she could see them wondering who she and the twins were, trying to place them. This was a small town, and outsiders stood out.

She hadn't always been a stranger here. She wondered how long it would take before somebody figured that out and remembered the last time Emily Elliott had been downtown in Pine Valley. That had been the day her grandmother had marched her into Donaldson's Drugstore to buy a home pregnancy test.

She'd felt pretty conspicuous then, too.

Emily's eyes flickered to the twins, who were clambering over the twisting roots of the ancient magnolia, and she felt her nerves ease a little. That had been the beginning of the toughest time in her life, but God had brought two amazing blessings out of it. He'd get her through today, too.

"I'm telling you, this isn't right." An emphatic male voice broke into Emily's thoughts, and she glanced up to see two men rounding the corner of the courthouse. "None of it's right."

Emily frowned. The man had his dark head turned away from her, but his voice sounded oddly familiar. He was tall and casually dressed in jeans and a red cotton shirt with the sleeves rolled up. His companion was older, and either the Georgia heat or the sharp edge of the tall man's voice had the fancy-dressed gentleman sweating through his very expensive suit.

"You're the lawyer," the familiar-sounding man continued. "Find a loophole."

"There isn't one." The other man mopped at his balding head with a handkerchief as he struggled to keep up with his companion's long strides. "We've been over this, Mr. Whitlock. Repeatedly. And all I can do is tell you the same thing I've been saying all along. There's nothing I can do."

Whitlock.

Emily squinted at the dark-haired man, and her heart jumped. She stood, shading her eyes with one hand to get a better look. "Abel? Abel Whitlock?"

The man stopped walking and turned toward her. "Emily?"

She felt her lips tilt upward in her first real smile in two long weeks. She took four running steps and flung herself into the tall man's arms hard enough that he staggered backward a step.

For a second she held on to him without thinking, her nose buried in the softness of his shirt, inhaling the scent of him—wood shavings, soap, the wild tang of the pine woods that surrounded his cabin. "Oh, it's so *good* to see a friendly face." She backed up a step, still clutching his upper arms, feeling the solid strength of his muscles through the worn cotton of his shirt. She peered up into his face. "You're a sight for sore eyes, you truly are!"

His blue eyes, startling in his tanned face, looked bemused. He seemed at a loss for words, but that wasn't unusual for Abel. She'd met him when she was fourteen, and he was the lanky eighteen-year-old who helped out on her grandmother's farm. He hadn't been much of a talker back then, either.

"Emily," he repeated.

She laughed self-consciously and released him. "I know. I'm terrible, flinging myself at you like that. I just couldn't help it." She turned back and motioned for her twins to approach them. "Phoebe, Paul, this is Grandma Sadie's friend Mr. Abel. He takes care of her animals." She smiled up at him. "He and I knew each other when I used to spend my summers with Grandma Sadie out on the farm."

The twins approached them slowly. Their experience with men in general was fairly limited—Emily didn't trust most men around her children. But this was Abel Whitlock, and he was in a category all by himself.

Abel detached his gaze from her face and dropped his eyes to the two tousled blond heads beside her.

"Well, now." He lowered himself slowly onto one knee and considered the children soberly. "So you're the famous twins I've heard so much about! I've waited a good while to meet you." He fished in his shirt pocket and produced a couple of striped discs of candy. "Do you like peppermint?"

Emily's smile widened. She'd seen him use the same technique countless times with skittish animals. *Move slow, talk low and have a treat ready*, he used to tell her. *They'll come around.*

The children considered his offering warily, glancing up at their mother for direction.

"You can take it. Mr. Abel's a good friend."

"You're big. Like a tree." Phoebe blinked her green eyes at him as she accepted her candy. Abel's mouth crooked up in a lopsided smile that jarred half a dozen more memories loose in Emily's mind. How could just that sideways quirk of his lips bring back so sharply the details of her Pine Valley summers? She could almost smell the odors of drying hay, fresh sliced tomatoes and green beans processing in her grandmother's pressure canner.

"I am that," Abel said, agreeing with her daughter. "And you're sweet. Like a daisy."

"She's not sweet all the time." Paul popped his own peppermint in his mouth and held out his hand. "I'm Paul Thomas Elliott, and it's nice to meet you. Thanks for the candy."

Abel shook the proffered hand. "I'm honored to meet you, sir, and you're welcome."

"I'm not a sir. Not yet. I'm just a kid." Paul cocked his head on one side, and Emily could see him weighing her old friend carefully. "But when I am a grown-up, I want to be a pilot. Of an airplane. Or maybe a rocket. I haven't decided yet." Emily smiled. Abel must have passed inspection. Paul was her reserved child, and he didn't share personal information easily.

"Good to know," Abel said gravely. "I like a man with a plan."

They nodded solemnly at each other for a couple of seconds before Abel got back to his feet. When his blue gaze returned to Emily's, it held a lingering gentleness that made inexplicable tears prick at the back of her eyes. She blinked furiously and managed to keep them from spilling over. Good grief. She was crying over everything these days.

Abel held his hand out to her next. "I didn't get a chance to speak to you at the funeral. I want you to know how sorry I am about Miss Sadie."

"You of all people don't have to tell me that." She took the hand he offered, feeling the dry roughness of his calloused skin. She squeezed hard, looking up into his face. "Grandma's death is just as much your loss as mine. I know that."

"Now, see there!" the stocky man interjected jovially. "It's always nice when folks get along. And it sure makes my job a whole lot easier." He offered his own hand to Emily. "Jim Monroe. And you must be Miss Elliott."

Her grandmother's lawyer. Finally. "Yes." She took the man's perspiring hand briefly in her own and couldn't help comparing its flabby softness to the hard strength of Abel's.

"I'm late, I know. Sorry about that. I was—" the man glanced up at Abel briefly before finishing "—delayed. Whew, it's hot as blazes out here! Why don't we take this little reunion inside where it's air-conditioned? The three of us have a lot to talk about."

Inside the lawyer's office Abel shifted his weight in the captain's chair he'd been assigned, and it creaked irritably. He ran a fingertip along its polished arm, assessing the wood. Cherry, he thought absently, with a pretty, rosy grain to it.

Any other day he'd have offered Monroe cash for this chair and hauled it back to his cabin. He'd have taken it apart, stripped off its polish and studied the grain of the wood, looking for the secrets he could carve out of it. But not today. Today he had other things on his mind.

Abel stole a look at Emily, who was standing at the doorway of the conference room talking earnestly to her twins. She was wearing a white shirt with short, filmy sleeves and pale green slacks, and she had that bright hair of hers pulled into some sort of soft little roll at the back of her neck. She was leaning over with her slim, city-pale arms extended, her hands resting gently on her twins' shoulders.

She reminded him of a dogwood tree just coming into blossom in the earliest days of spring, when its flowering branches looked like bits of lace tangled in the pines. Emily had always had something of the refreshing chanciness of springtime about her, and she'd always given Abel the same fluttering, uncertain feeling in his belly that the first days of March always did. That sense of waking up after the dull darkness of winter.

When she'd run up and grabbed him outside, he'd felt just like he had last fall when Miss Sadie's ornery little bull calf butted him squarely in the stomach. But then Emily'd always had a knack for knocking him off balance, for making him feel clumsy and foolish, like he was wearing his boots on the wrong feet. Back when she spent her summers on Goosefeather Farm, he'd done his share of mooning over her.

That was what happened when you put a lonesome boy and a pretty girl in the same general vicinity, he reckoned. Of course, Emily had never looked twice in his direction, not that way, and he'd never seriously expected her to. The Whitlock and Elliott properties might butt up against each other, but the families were worlds apart in every other way. Even back then, he'd had enough sense to know that much.

All that was water under an old bridge, because once Emily heard what this lawyer had to say, Abel didn't figure on getting another hug from her any time soon.

"You be good for Miss Marianne, now," Emily was telling her children. "Mind your manners."

"I always mind my manners," the boy, Paul, answered in a matter-of-fact tone. "It's Phoebe who forgets."

"I do not! Well…" Phoebe stuck one finger between her pink lips and hesitated. "*Sometimes* I forget." In spite of the knot of nerves in his belly, Abel found himself smiling.

Emily's twins were cute little things with bright expressions and golden hair exactly the color of wildflower honey, just like their mama's. The boy had Trey Gordon's brown eyes, though, and the girl had something of Trey in the set of her chin.

The memory of Trey Gordon made the smile fade from Abel's face. The summer that Emily Elliott had fallen for Trey had been her last in Pine Valley, and the recollection of it still rankled more than he liked to admit. Still, the man was dead and gone. If Abel couldn't bring himself to be overly sorry about that, at least with the good Lord's help he could toss a little mercy at Trey's memory.

Miss Sadie had taught him that much.

"The kids will be fine." Jim Monroe sounded impatient. "Marianne loves kids, don't you, Marianne? Take 'em down the hall to the library, and let them watch cartoons on the television in there." Monroe dismissed his secretary with a wave and began rummaging through the files stacked on his desk. "Have a seat, Miss Elliott, and we'll get started."

Emily had her head stuck out into the hallway, watching her children. She glanced at the lawyer, but she lingered where she was, apparently reluctant to let her children out of her sight.

She's a good mother, Abel realized, which was pretty remarkable considering that her own mother hadn't exactly been cut out for parenthood. He'd only met Marlene Elliott a few times, but he remembered her as a flighty woman who always seemed to be in the middle of some kind of man-related crisis. Maybe Emily had inherited her common sense from Tom Elliott, Miss Sadie's son. He'd passed on before Abel came into the picture, but Tom was remembered in Pine Valley as a solid, upstanding man.

"Close the door if you would, Miss Elliott." The lawyer darted an uneasy look at Abel. "In these situations privacy is important."

Emily hesitated another second, then eased the heavy door shut. She came over to take her place in the second chair angled across from the lawyer's desk.

"Now, Mr. Whitlock, Miss Elliott, you're here because you are both beneficiaries of Mrs. Sadie Elliott's last will and testament."

Abel's heart sank, and he glanced over at Emily wondering how she'd take this first blow. Emily turned to him, her face lighting up like a spring sunrise.

"Oh, Abel. I'm so glad! You've been such a help to Grandma all these years. She'd never have been able to stay on Goosefeather Farm without you, and we both know she'd have been miserable anywhere else. I'm so happy she remembered you in her will!"

Abel winced. He'd thought he couldn't feel any worse about this whole thing than he already did.

He'd been wrong.

"I never expected her to." Abel cut another look at Jim Monroe, who winced and pulled a tissue out of the box on his desk to dab at his perspiring forehead. "And, Emily, I want you to know before we go any further, that I had nothing to do with this."

"We've been through all that, Mr. Whitlock," Monroe sighed heavily and continued as if Abel had directed his comment toward him. "I'm well aware of your sentiments on the matter. But as I've already explained to you, Mrs. Elliott set out her wishes very clearly in her will, and like it or not, all three of us are going to have to abide by her terms or accept the consequences."

Emily frowned. "Of course we'll abide by the terms of Grandma's will. Why wouldn't we?" She looked from one man to the other, her expression puzzled. "What consequences are you talking about? What's going on?"

Fifteen minutes later she knew.

"You have *got* to be kidding me." Emily sounded bewildered, but she didn't sound angry. Not yet. Abel had his elbows on the desk and his chin cradled in his hands.

So far this was going just about the way he'd figured it would. Not well.

"I'm afraid it's no joke, Miss Elliott." Jim Monroe slid his glasses down his nose and looked at Emily sympathetically. "As I said, Mrs. Elliott was very clear. Either you reside on Goosefeather Farm for three months and care for its livestock and crops to the satisfaction of the county extension agent, beginning now, or you forfeit the farm and the rest of your grandmother's assets to Mr. Whitlock here. Lock, stock and barrel."

Abel's gut clenched. Emily was pale except for two spots of red burning high on each cheekbone. She looked like she'd just been slapped.

He couldn't have loved Miss Sadie Elliott any more if she'd been his own flesh and blood, which was no wonder when you considered that she'd done a sight more for him than any of his own people ever had. When she'd died it had felt like somebody had cut a chunk right out of the middle of his heart. But she'd sure left him in a mess with this crazy notion of hers.

"I can't live here!" Emily was protesting. "I have a job and an apartment in Atlanta. Phoebe and Paul will be starting kindergarten in August. I've already registered them." She shook her head. "I just don't get it. What was Grandma thinking?"

"As it happens, we may have an answer to that question." Jim Monroe slipped an envelope out from under the papers neatly stacked in the manila folder in front of him. He slid it across the table toward Emily. "She left this for you."

Emily accepted the letter, which bore her name in Miss Sadie's spidery writing, but she kept her eyes fixed imploringly on the lawyer. "You don't understand. I can't stay in Pine Valley," she repeated. "I just can't!"

"If you're unable to meet the conditions of the will, then I'm afraid Mr. Whitlock gets the farm and all your grandmother's monetary assets, which while hardly extensive are not inconsequential. I'm very sorry, Miss Elliot. I can see this wasn't what you were expecting, and I agree that it's quite unusual. I also want you to know that I did encourage Mrs. Elliott to speak to you about it when we drew up the will a couple of years ago. Obviously she didn't take my advice."

"This is crazy." Emily closed her eyes and rubbed her temples with trembling fingers. "I don't know what I'm supposed to do." The confusion and hurt on her face reminded Abel of the time he'd happened across a tiny fawn tangled up in the rusty remains of a barbed-wire fence. Emily's expression tore into his heart just the same way. Only this time he couldn't ease the pain with a pair of wire cutters and some salve.

Monroe coughed. "Miss Elliott, this isn't a decision to be made in haste. Read your grandmother's letter and think things over. You can come by tomorrow and let me know what you decide. "

"I was going back to Atlanta this afternoon. I have to work a double shift tomorrow. It's the only way I could get today off."

The lawyer made a sympathetic noise as he got up from the table. "Here's your copy of the will, Miss Elliott. And yours, Mr. Whitlock. Should you have any questions, you can give me a call. But as I've already explained to Mr. Whitlock at some length, this will's going to hold. I drew it up myself, and I know my business. You're welcome to consult with another lawyer if you choose to fight it, but if he's worth his salt he'll tell you the same thing."

And charge you a pretty penny to do so, Abel thought grimly. He'd already called another attorney, and he'd gotten nowhere.

Monroe shook both their hands. "Take your time if you want to discuss it. The children are fine with Marianne." He nodded and then exited his office with an air of relief, pulling the door carefully shut behind him.

The silence in the room was leaden. Emily wouldn't look in Abel's direction.

"Did you know about all this?" she asked finally, keeping her gaze on the hands she held tightly in her lap.

"Not until it was too late to do anything about it. Monroe called me the day after Miss Sadie passed and told me the basics." He'd been looking for loopholes ever since, but he hadn't found any, so he saw no sense in mentioning that.

"Mr. Monroe didn't tell me anything over the phone except that Grandma left some special condition in the will. I thought it had something to do with finding new homes for the livestock. You know how she was about her animals. I never imagined..." Emily massaged her temples again. "I wasn't expecting anything like this. Mr. Monroe should have given me the same information he gave you so I could have been prepared."

"He was probably afraid to," Abel said honestly. "I've been giving him kind of a hard time about all this." The truth was, he'd hounded the life out of the lawyer, desperate to avoid this very moment. The look on Emily's face made him wish he'd tried a little harder, although he didn't see how he could have.

"Really?" Emily's voice chilled. "Why would you do that? As it stands, all you have to do is wait for me to fail, and you end up with Grandma's farm. You've always been crazy about the place. It seems to me this is a pretty sweet deal for you."

His heart dropped to the bottom of his gut. This was exactly what he'd been afraid of, what had kept him awake half of last night. He'd worried she'd think he'd finagled this somehow, that he was the kind of person who'd have conned an elderly lady into something like this.

She wouldn't be alone in thinking it, either, and for

good reason. He was the son of a man like that and the grandson of another one. He'd worked hard to build a different kind of reputation for himself in Pine Valley, but it had been uphill work. Easier, his younger brother, Danny, had said, just to move off and start fresh in a place where the Whitlock name wasn't muddied up with generations of lies, bad debts and shady deals.

Abel had argued, but Danny had had his heart jammed up by some girl who'd looked down her nose at him and he'd been in no mood to listen. His brother had left, and Abel had set his jaw and started the long, slow work of forging trust with his wary neighbors. One day Danny would feel the call of home. Everybody did, sooner or later. And when that day came, he was going to find out that the Whitlocks had a different reputation in this town. Abel intended to make sure of that, and he'd come too far to see it all crumble into dust just because Miss Sadie had come up with one of her crazy ideas.

He met Emily's eyes squarely. "I've already told you I had nothing to do with any of this. If I wanted Goose-feather Farm, I'd have asked Miss Sadie to sell it to me and given her a fair price for it. I'd have asked her straight out, too, like a decent man does when he wants something. I would never have gone behind your back and wheedled her into giving it to me and shortchanging yo—" He stopped short when he saw Emily's bottom lip trembling. He was about to make her cry, which was just about the only thing that would make this situation even worse than it already was.

"Emily," he began helplessly but then floundered. He had no idea what to say. Words never came easily to him, and this was way beyond his skill level.

She got up, pushing her chair back so abruptly it almost tilted over. "I can't talk about this right now. I've got to find somewhere to think…and to read this letter. I've got to make sense of this somehow."

Abel reached deep in his jeans pocket, pulling out an old-fashioned key. "Here. Why don't you go out to the farm? I've been locking up since…for the last couple of weeks and taking care of things."

Emily's eyes flashed angrily, and her chin went up a notch. "I already have a key, thanks. It was my grandmother's house after all."

Abel winced. He was trying to help, but he'd managed to put his foot in it instead. He felt like he was trying to plow a field blindfolded.

"Emily," he tried again, but she cut him off firmly.

"Don't try to talk to me right now, Abel, please. Just don't. I'm tired, and I've got a lot to think about. You and I've known each other for a long time, and you were always nice to me when I came out for the summers. You looked out for me, and I haven't forgotten that. You even used to sneak around and do my chores sometimes when Grandma wasn't looking." A smile flickered briefly on her lips. "You're probably the only friend I have left around here. I really—" Her voice broke again, and she coughed and restarted. "I really don't want to say something to you right now that I'll regret later." Her voice sounded thick, but whether it was clogged with tears or anger, he couldn't tell.

He sat like a stone, listening as she went down the carpeted hallway and gathered up her twins, who protested at leaving in the middle of their cartoon. He waited until he heard the outer office door shut solidly behind her. Then he sighed and rubbed wearily at his eyes.

He had no idea what Miss Sadie had been thinking, but surely this wasn't what she'd been hoping for. Emily was hurt and angry, and Abel felt like he'd just murdered a puppy. And he had a hunch things were going to get a whole lot trickier before they got any better. If they ever did.

He got to his feet, folding up his copy of the will into a square that would fit in his shirt pocket. He was anxious to escape this stuffy office and get back outside, where he could breathe. Emily wasn't the only one who needed to think. Maybe a walk in the woods and some time in his workshop would clear his head. He'd spend some more time praying, too. He always felt closer to God out alone under the pines or with his chisel in his hand than he did indoors crowded up next to other folks. It was something he'd had a hard time explaining to the new minister when he'd pestered Abel gently about his spotty church attendance.

Yes, he'd have another long talk with God. Maybe this time the good Lord would give him some clear instructions about how to handle all this. He sure hoped so, because Abel was going to need all the help he could get.

Chapter Two

Phoebe fell asleep on the ten-minute ride out to Goose-feather Farm and had to be wakened when they pulled up in front of the white farmhouse. Even Paul's eyelids looked a bit heavy, and he leaned against the clapboards on the shady porch as Emily twisted the metal key in the ancient lock. She was a little surprised when she heard the tumblers click grudgingly back into place. Although her grandmother had given her the key several years ago, Emily had never actually used it. The truth was she'd never known this welcoming red door to be locked, and she was amazed that the key even worked.

She gave the children a snack of apple wedges and cheese at her grandmother's big kitchen table and then took them upstairs and settled them in the spare bedroom for a nap. It was proof of their exhaustion that they accepted this arrangement without a fuss. Phoebe flopped on top of the blue-and-yellow quilt covering the bed nearest the window, cuddled her tattered stuffed rabbit close to her, sighed once and promptly fell back asleep. Paul arranged himself more carefully in the other twin bed, tracing the pointed stars of his matching quilt with a thoughtful finger.

"Are you going to take a nap, too, Mama?" he asked.

She wished. "No. I've got some thinking to do."

"Oh." He nodded sagely. "But thinking's hard work, and you're tired. You might better rest awhile first." After that pronouncement he closed his eyes and stuck his thumb in his mouth.

Emily kissed him gently, smiling at her son's unique mixture of innocence and maturity. His preschool teachers had already labeled Paul gifted. That might explain why he often seemed so much older than his years. Emily still worried that being the son of a single mom was making her little boy grow up too fast. His manly little efforts to take care of his mother and sister made her both proud and sad.

She left the door to the twins' room ajar and crossed the hall to the bedroom that had been hers. Like the rest of the old-fashioned farmhouse, it hadn't changed much in the last six years. Its generous windows faced west, and the early-afternoon sun slanted warmly across the wide oak floorboards. The violet-sprigged curtains were the ones her grandmother had let her choose from a catalogue years ago. Now they were looped back with faded lavender ribbons to show off a view of the farm's rolling fields and trim little barns. Emily's books were still lined up on the white shelf underneath the window, and her teacup collection was arranged along the wide windowsill. Outside this room, Emily's life had rushed forward like a runaway train, but in here time had held its breath.

She doubted her grandmother had left things this way because of sentimentality. Grandma had just been allergic to change, and she'd never paid much attention to the inside of the house anyway. Sadie Elliott had always preferred to be outside spoiling one of her beloved animals or puttering around in her garden. She'd never known quite what to do with her indoorsy granddaughter, but Sadie had still insisted on the annual visits, rightly guessing that Emily's mother was far too busy chasing men to supervise her daughter during her school vacation. And while Emily had never particularly enjoyed spending her summers on the farm, she'd grown to love her outspoken grandmother fiercely.

She could remember exactly where she'd been standing in the coffee shop when Mr. Alvarez relayed the message that her grandmother had died. Emily had dropped the metal tray she'd been sliding into the glass showcase, and muffins had rolled in every direction. Caramel pecan, the Tuesday special. When she got her next paycheck, she'd discovered that Mr. Alvarez had docked her pay to cover the cost of the dropped muffins. Compassion wasn't her boss's strongest trait. If she stayed on the farm for the summer, she'd almost certainly lose her job.

If she stayed. She couldn't believe she was even considering it. She rummaged in her purse and brought out her cell phone. Forcing herself not to think about the minutes she was squandering, she sank down on the white chenille bedspread and dialed her friend Clary Wright's number.

Clary answered on the first ring. "Well," she said, "you're using your cell phone, so I already know this is something big. Either your grandmother was secretly a millionaire and left you wads of money, or that rattletrap car of yours conked out and you need your roomie from the big city to drive to the boonies and rescue the three of you. Which is it?"

Emily felt her lips tilting up at her friend's familiar voice. Clary was just what she needed right now. "Neither one. Right now I really just need a listening ear."

"Uh-oh. You must need one pretty badly to be using those precious minutes of yours. What's up?"

Clary listened as Emily filled her in on the terms of the will. "Wow. So, what did the letter say?"

"I haven't opened it yet." Emily glanced at the envelope lying beside her on the bedspread. "I think… I think I'd like to make up my own mind about what I want to do before I read it. That's why I called. I don't have a clue what I'm supposed to do here, Clary."

"Now that's a switch." Clary's laugh bubbled through the phone. "You've never had much trouble knowing your own mind, Em. I'm always the one calling you."

"Well, this isn't exactly an easy choice." Emily glanced out the window at the tidy barnyard. "On the one hand this could make a real difference for the twins and me. Financially, I mean. There's over a hundred acres here, not to mention the farmhouse and the barns. I have no idea how much it'd sell for, but…"

"Whatever it is, it's a lot more than you've got right now," Clary finished for her. "You've been praying for the money to start up your own coffee shop, Em. Maybe this is the answer you've been waiting for."

Emily had thought of that, too. "It's possible, I guess. But it seems like a pretty strange way for God to answer. I stink at farming."

"You only have to hold things together for the summer. How hard can it be?"

How hard can it be? Emily wanted to laugh, but

it really wasn't funny. "Harder than you can imagine. You've never lived in the country, Clary. You don't know about farms."

"Maybe not, but I know about you. You're a working single mom of twins, Emily! Farming should be a snap compared to that."

"But if I stay here for the whole summer, I'll lose my job at Café Cup for sure."

"True," Clary admitted after a thoughtful second. "But you know, maybe that wouldn't be such a bad thing. Mr. Alvarez takes advantage of you."

Emily sighed. Clary, who tended to flit from job to job, had worked at Café Cup herself. Her accident-prone nature and the boss's skinflinty tendencies hadn't been a good combination. "You just don't like him because he fired you."

"Not true. I don't hold grudges. You know that. No, this is all about you. How many of your muffin recipes are on his menu now? Five?"

"Six."

"And aren't those his best sellers?"

"Usually." Emily felt a tiny flush of satisfaction.

"But he pays you the same as the other waitresses, right? Even though you're creating these unique recipes and baking half his product? I'm not sure I'd pass up this opportunity just to keep a job like that."

"But if I lose my job, how can I pay my half of our rent?" Emily felt panicky just thinking about it.

"Don't worry about that. I can stretch my budget a little bit and handle the rent by myself for a while."

"I can't ask you to do that."

"You didn't ask. You never do. And this time I'm not taking no for an answer. Listen." Clary's soft voice took on an uncharacteristic firmness. "You can do this, Em. I know you can! And what's more, I know you'll never forgive yourself if you don't at least try."

Clary had a point. Emily ended the call and set the phone down on the snowy bedspread. Well, she couldn't put this off forever. She took one steadying breath and tore up the envelope's flap.

Her grandmother's message was written in blue ball-point pen on a plain sheet of notebook paper. Sadie Elliott had never been one for frills or preambles. She got right to the point.

I know right now you're probably pretty hot at me, but you're just going to have to get over it.

You're not much on trusting folks, Emily-girl, and I understand that. But you're going to have to trust me on this one thing. I had my reasons for leaving things the way I did. Believe it or not, I did it because I love you, and I want what's best for you. And like all old folks, I think I've got a better idea of what that is than you do, so I couldn't resist taking one last opportunity to meddle a little.

You've got plenty of spunk and grit in you, Emily. I admire that—probably because you got those things from me. You're also stubborn as a country mule. That part you got from your grandpa. When that man made up his mind about something, he was harder to move than a sack of bees.

You settled on an opinion about Pine Valley and Goosefeather Farm a long time ago, and I don't think you gave either of them a fair shake. I always felt like you were made and meant for this old place, but you were too bullheaded to consider its good points and too busy mooning after the likes of Trey Gordon to notice what the good Lord put right under that pretty little nose of yours.

But there's no point my going into all that now. Anyhow, it's something you'll have to figure out for yourself.

Maybe you're right, and you never belonged here. Then again maybe you're wrong. You know well enough what I always thought. Here's your chance to find out once and for all which one of us is right.

As usual, I'm banking on me. I'm not much to look at, but I'm smart as a whip.

Praying God's blessings on you and those sweet babies.

All my love,
Grandma

While she was reading, the tears Emily had been fighting all day had spattered down on her grandmother's writing, making wet circles on the paper. She'd heard her grandmother's voice just as plainly as if the feisty old lady had been sitting next to her.

She folded up the letter carefully and slipped it back into its envelope. She sat on the bed for a few minutes listening to the ponderous ticking of the grandfather clock at the base of the stairs and the occasional squawk of a chicken from the barnyard.

When nineteen-year-old Emily's pregnancy test had come up positive, Grandma had set her lips together tightly and left the room for fifteen minutes. When she returned, she'd given her granddaughter a fierce hug and told her she was welcome to stay at Goosefeather Farm for as long as she liked. They'd raise the baby together with God's help.

She'd never understood Emily's unwillingness to take her up on that offer, and she hadn't approved of Emily's choice to return to Atlanta. Sadie's concerns turned out to be right on target. When Emily got back to her mother's apartment, she discovered that Marlene had followed her latest boyfriend to Florida, leaving nothing behind but a stack of overdue bills and a scribbled note saying that Emily was plenty old enough to manage on her own. If Sadie had known half of what Emily had gone through during her first months alone in the city, her grandmother would have driven her old Ford truck up there and hauled her granddaughter straight back to Pine Valley.

Sadie Elliott had been an independent woman herself, though, and she'd reluctantly allowed Emily to forge her own path. Still she'd never really understood why Emily was so stubborn in her refusal to return to Pine Valley or why Emily had gone to such great lengths to entice her grandmother up to Atlanta for holidays and birthday celebrations. Sadie had felt Emily was being unreasonable, and she'd said so on several occasions.

But Grandma hadn't known everything.

Before Emily had gone to her grandmother with her suspicions, she'd already been to speak to Trey Gordon and his widowed mother, Lois. Naive as she'd been back then, Emily had banked on Trey's boyish promises, and she'd confidently expected to be making wedding plans once the initial shock subsided.

Instead Trey's socially prominent mother had wasted

no time setting Emily straight. There would be no marriage. Her son's bright future wasn't going to be dimmed by tying himself to the likes of Emily Elliott, no matter what kind of fix she'd managed to get herself in. In Lois's opinion Emily's best option was to take herself and her problems back up to Atlanta. Given the sort of woman Emily's mother was, Lois had no doubt Marlene would know how to deal with this. Trey had simply sat by without saying a word, letting his mother fillet Emily into quivering strips with her barbed tongue.

Trey had been killed in a drunk driving accident over four years ago, but apparently his mother had never forgiven Emily for having the audacity to expect her precious son to shoulder his rightful responsibilities. Lois had made that perfectly clear when she bumped into Emily on the morning of Sadie Elliott's funeral. Emily had felt the chill radiating off Trey's mother from all the way across the room, and it had been a profound relief when she'd finally been able to put Pine Valley in her rearview mirror and head back to the haven of the Atlanta apartment she and the twins shared with Clary.

Now she was supposed to stay here for the whole summer? It was a daunting thought.

She got to her feet and crossed over the creaking floor to the window that looked out over the farm. She could see her grandma's milk cow grazing placidly in the pasture on the right-hand side of the house and the vegetable garden to the left with its tidy rows. The far field was dotted with black Angus cows. They were the farm's bread and butter and depended on the hay fields, which were tucked out of sight behind the house.

It all looked so serene and orderly. Emily knew it was anything but.

Already weeds were impudently sprouting up between the plants in the garden, and each row of vegetables would end up requiring hours of labor before the produce made it to the local farmers' market or to the farmhouse kitchen, where it would have to be processed and canned to be stored for winter eating. That cow would have to be milked night and morning no matter what else was going on, and the dairy pails and strainers would have to be scrubbed and sanitized daily. Those black Angus cows would need to be carefully monitored and fed if they were going to bring top price at the end of the summer. Then there were the goats and the chickens to look after.

And the hay field. Emily didn't even want to think about that hay field. Haying was backbreaking work that required the use of a lot of complicated equipment that she couldn't even imagine running on her own. She didn't know much about any of this. She'd spent most of her summers on the farm trying to avoid this type of work so she could spend her time tinkering around in her grandma's old-fashioned kitchen. And now she had the twins to look after, as well.

Her grandma had always counted on Abel Whitlock to do the toughest farm work, but Emily could hardly expect him to help out now, not when he stood to inherit the place if she made a mess of things. Besides, even if he were willing, she had no money to pay him.

She might as well face it. She was on her own. And that was fine, she told herself, lifting her chin a fraction. She was better off that way. Depending on other people was what generally got her in trouble.

Through the window Emily watched a hen that had somehow managed to escape from the coop, wandering the yard, clucking and pecking at bugs. She'd have to catch the silly bird before a hawk did and then try to block the hole in the chicken pen. She'd have to see the rest of the animals settled for the night, too, which meant she was going to have to take her first shot at milking a cow in years.

Then she'd have to go back to Atlanta and do her best to explain things to Mr. Alvarez. Given her boss's temperament, she knew keeping her job was unlikely, but she'd see what she could do. She needed that job.

Because the minute the farm was legally hers, Emily planned to stick a for-sale sign in the yard, point her little car back toward Atlanta, and once again put Pine Valley and all its painful memories in her rearview mirror—this time permanently. For once in her life, Sadie Elliott had gotten things utterly and completely wrong.

Emily didn't belong on Goosefeather Farm. She never had, and she never would.

Abel rounded the corner of Miss Sadie's barn and stopped short in the wide doorway. Beulah the cow was clumsily tied into her stanchion, and Emily was crouched down beside her, trying to poke the stainless steel milking pail under the bulging udder. The twins were standing a respectful distance away watching the process with doubtful expressions.

For a moment Abel was distracted by the picture they made. The fading sunlight reached through the slats of the barn wall to highlight Emily's honey-colored hair, which was gathered into a messy knot on the top of her head. The twins were mostly in shadow with only their faces picking up the light.

Abel's fingers itched for a sketch pad. There was so

much here he could carve: the curves of Emily's face, the sturdy, childish shapes of the twins...

The cow shifted irritably. Abel blinked, and his mind shifted abruptly back into gear. "Emily, look out there! You're on the wrong side. She's going to kick you!"

As if on cue the Jersey lifted one fawn-colored leg and struck out sideways in Emily's direction. Emily fell backward, her breath escaping her in a loud huff, while Beulah focused on aiming her second kick at the empty pail.

The pail landed next to Emily with a loud clang that set the hens clucking worriedly. Abel crossed the barn in three strides and knelt down beside Emily, whose gray-green eyes were wide.

"Did she get you?" Abel asked as he helped Emily back to her feet. "She can be an ornery old girl. You have to watch her."

"I'm all right." She stepped away from him, dusting off her pants with quick, irritated motions. "Stupid cow."

"Beulah's smart enough. That's the problem. If she was stupid, she'd be a lot easier to handle." Since Emily seemed unhurt, Abel turned his attention to the cow. He placed a reassuring hand on Beulah's flank and murmured to her, settling her with his familiar touch and voice. The Jersey gave a long-suffering sigh and rolled her big brown eyes reproachfully in his direction. *About time you showed up*, she seemed to be saying.

He almost hadn't come at all. He'd dawdled a full forty-five minutes after his normal chore time wondering if he should. In the end his concern for the animals had won out. Emily didn't know the routines, and she didn't know where the feed was. He didn't know if she wanted his help or not, but he knew she needed it. So, like it or not, she was going to get it.

"Maybe I'd better milk her out for you tonight." He righted the toppled pail with one hand and scooped up the three-legged milking stool with the other. "Cows are kind of particular about their milking routine, Beulah more than most," he explained, stepping over to the other side of the fidgeting cow. "She'll probably behave herself better for somebody she's used to." As he settled in on the correct side, he could feel the cow relaxing. She took up a mouthful of grain and began crunching calmly, looking as if she'd never tried to kick anybody in her life.

Abel, on the other hand, felt as jumpy as a cricket in a henhouse…and a whole lot less welcomed. Emily was still standing in the spot where he'd left her, and the twins, their eyes big with curiosity, were watching him clean off Beulah's full udder with the wipes Miss Sadie kept on hand.

Abel had never spent much time around kids, and the few he'd run into here and there hadn't left all that favorable an impression. These two seemed different. He liked the no-nonsense way the boy had of summing things up, and Emily's little girl had a real special sparkle to her.

He liked them just fine, but that didn't mean he knew how to talk to them. It didn't help matters that they kept staring at him wide-eyed like two tawny little owls. Fortunately for Abel, milking was a great way to avoid eye contact. He kept his gaze focused on the streams of creamy liquid that jetted into the bucket with a ringing hiss as his practiced hands did their work.

Paul walked over and hunkered down next to him,

watching the process with a wrinkled nose. "I don't think I like milk anymore."

"Me, either," said Phoebe, who was keeping a safe distance.

"Aw, now. You'll hurt Beulah's feelings talking like that. Anyhow, I expect you'll change your mind when you taste this milk. Beulah's milk is the best in the county, maybe even the state. You'll see."

"Paul, back up. I don't want that cow to kick you." Emily sounded irked.

"He's all right. She's not in a kicking mood anymore," Abel said evenly. "She was just reminding you that cows like to be milked from the right, that's all."

"How does a cow know the difference between right and left?" Paul was skeptical. "Even Phoebe doesn't know that yet."

"I do, too, know that!"

"You don't, either."

"Children." Emily's voice held a tinge of desperation. "Why don't you go look at the chickens for a few minutes and let me speak to Mr. Abel?"

"Chicken feed's in that big metal can over there. You can throw some to 'em if you want to," Abel suggested. The twins scurried off excitedly.

"Stay outside the pen," Emily called. "That rooster might be mean."

"He is that," Abel agreed. "Newman's about the meanest rooster I've ever seen. Your grandma was the only one who could handle him."

Emily fixed him with chilly eyes. "What are you doing here, Abel?"

"It's milking time. I thought you might need a hand."

He'd been right, but he figured it was the better part of wisdom not to point that out.

"I can manage on my own." Emily tilted up her chin as if daring him to argue with her.

He wasn't going to. According to the information that had filtered down through Miss Sadie to him over the last six years, managing on her own was Emily's specialty. This woman had plenty of grit. She was just a little low on know-how.

And maybe gratitude, come to think of it.

"I'm not saying you can't handle things by yourself, but it's been a while since you had to deal with this kind of stuff, and now you've got twins to look after in the bargain. I know the ropes around Goosefeather, and your grandma was good to me. I'm just trying to help you out a little."

"Yes, well. Your helping me is kind of a conflict of interest right now, isn't it?"

Abel felt temper flare inside him. The tempo of his milking upped a little, but he kept his voice carefully calm. "Not the way I see it, no." There was a pause, punctuated by the hiss of the milk foaming in the half-full bucket and the excited clucking of the hens as Paul and Phoebe tossed cracked corn through the chicken wire.

Emily sighed sharply. "I just don't think this is a wise move right now, Abel. Your helping, I mean."

"That kind of depends on what you call wise, I guess," Abel said, stripping the last drops of milk from Beulah's deflated udder. He lifted the heavy pail from under the cow's belly and topped it with its clean lid before setting it safely to the side. "Maybe you and I have different takes on it. Like right now it seems to me you're looking a gift horse in the mouth, and that sure doesn't seem all that smart to me." He angled himself under the cow and carefully applied the spray that would help protect her from mastitis.

"Sorry, but it's been my experience that gifts, horses or otherwise, tend to come with strings attached."

"Mama!" Phoebe's excited voice called over from the chicken pen. "Did you say *horse*? Is there a horsie here? I love horsies!"

"No, hon. No horsies," Emily called back.

"Can we get one? Please?"

"Good heavens, no! The last thing I need around here is something else to feed and look after," Emily added under her breath.

"You've got a lot on your plate all right," Abel agreed. "That's why I think it'd be foolish of you not to take what help you can get." He stood up, unhooked Beulah from her stanchion and gave her an affectionate slap on her bony rump as she ambled peaceably out of the barn to graze in the evening cool. "And just so you know, I don't do gifts with strings, Emily. Either I give them or I don't. Look, I know you're mad about how Miss Sadie left the will, and I can't say that I blame you. I'm none too happy about it, either."

"Yes. So you said."

There was something in her voice, some subtle tone of disbelief that jarred a little of his temper loose. It wasn't the first time somebody had distrusted him, far from it, but it sure stung coming from Emily Elliott of all people, here in the one place where he'd always been trusted and relied on in spite of his last name.

"It's the truth, but I reckon you can believe it or not as it suits you. That doesn't change the fact that you're going to need some help around here at least at the beginning. I'm willing to give it. If you're as smart as I think you are, you'll put your feelings about all this aside and take me up on it. Otherwise I think you're going to find yourself going under pretty quick."

Emily looked at him with her indecision written plainly on her face. She had an independent streak a mile wide, and apparently she'd gotten burned often enough not to trust people easily. Her suspicion was warring hard with her common sense, and from the look of things, it might take a while for the dust to settle there. In the meantime, Miss Sadie's animals were already about an hour behind their normal eating schedules. They'd wasted enough time as it was.

He had opened his mouth to say so when suddenly a bloodcurdling child's scream came from the direction of the chicken pen.

"Phoebe!" Emily bolted toward the noise.

"Newman!" Abel overtook Emily in two strides and was inside the chicken coop in a flash. He pushed himself between the five-year-old and the angry bantam and swept up the sobbing little girl in his arms.

"There, now," he said to Phoebe, keeping his eyes on the tiny rooster, who was stalking around in the corner of the coop, his bright feathers standing out in an angry halo. "It's all right. I've got you."

"He tried to claw me!" Phoebe snuffled moistly into Abel's neck.

"She went in to get an egg." Paul spoke from outside the pen, his voice shaking. "I told her not to, but she wouldn't listen. And then the rooster started chasing her and flying up at her!"

"He was protecting his hens. It's what good roosters

do. Newman's just not smart enough to figure out that you're not going to hurt them, is all."

"He's a bad, bad bird!" Phoebe peered around Abel's neck at the little rooster, who crowed fiercely and ruffled his feathers. Phoebe promptly buried her face again, and Abel felt her little hands tighten.

Something in his heart shifted strangely at the feel of those tiny fingers twisting in the fabric of his shirt, and Abel looked narrowly at the strutting rooster. Newman considered Abel's expression, and some primal warning must have flashed in his walnut-sized brain. He settled his feathers and sidled into the depths of his corner, edging behind a fat black-striped hen, who squawked at him irritably.

It looked like Newman was nobody's favorite today.

Emily was beside him now, tugging Phoebe free of his arms and carrying her out of the coop. She knelt down in front of her daughter and checked her over with worried hands.

"I think he just scared her." Abel shot another meaningful glance at the rooster, who meekly lowered his head and pretended to be interested in pecking at a piece of straw. Abel retrieved the egg that had caught Phoebe's attention and latched the coop door securely behind himself.

"That's why we told you *not* to go into the coop, young lady." Emily's voice was tense and stern. "You could have gotten hurt. That rooster could have put your eye out."

In spite of himself Abel couldn't help smiling a little. Emily was a mother all right. Mothers were always concerned about somebody putting an eye out. At least that was what he'd heard. Since his own mother had lit out when he was ten, he didn't have a whole lot of first-hand knowledge in that department.

"I wanted to get the egg," Phoebe wailed, fresh tears starting.

"And here it is. There'll be more of them come morning. Next time, though, you'd better wait and let me go in there with you. Okay?" Abel handed over the smooth brown egg, and the tears stopped instantly.

"I'm going to go put it in the 'frigerator!" she exclaimed happily, and she and Paul dashed out of the barn toward the house.

"If that egg makes it all the way into a carton, I'll be amazed," Emily muttered under her breath. Then she glanced up at Abel. "Thanks."

"No problem."

"I guess Grandma's rooster's made your point for you. That scared me to death. Doing the chores around here and keeping an eye on the twins at the same time… well, it's going to be a lot to manage. I couldn't live with myself if Paul or Phoebe got hurt because I wasn't paying attention."

She was probably overestimating the damage one pint-size rooster could have caused, but he figured it wouldn't be to his advantage to mention that. "Neither could I."

"I guess if your offer still stands…" She trailed off.

"It does."

"I don't know how we can work this out, though. I can't pay you. At least not until the farm sells."

Until the farm sells. The words stabbed at him, but he shoved the pain aside for the moment. "I'm not asking for any pay."

"Well, you're not working here for free. That's out of

the question." Emily's chin went up mulishly. She didn't want to be beholden to him. That was plain enough.

This was going nowhere fast, and he had hungry animals to tend to. "You'd better get on back in the house with the little ones. You've probably got some egg to clean up by now."

The distraction worked. A tiny smile tickled around the corners of her lips. "You're probably right."

"Here. Take this milk on in with you and get it strained and chilling. You remember how to do that, don't you?"

"Sure." Emily reached over and took the full pail he held out to her. He winced a little when he saw her adjust her slim frame to balance its heft. He should offer to carry it for her. He'd always brought the milk pails in for Miss Sadie.

But he had a feeling Emily needed to feel like she was carrying her weight, so he let it go. "While you're tending to that, I'll finish up with the animals. I'll come up to the kitchen for a minute or two when I'm done, and we'll hash out some kind of arrangement. All right?"

Emily hesitated. She'd never been much on being told what to do, but she finally gave in. "All right." She turned, carefully managing the milk bucket so it wouldn't slop over on her pants, and headed back toward the farmhouse.

Abel began to measure out feed to take to the goats in the west pasture. Judging by the level of pellets in the big can, he'd need to make another trip to the feed store soon. Beulah was running low on her alfalfa hay, too, and that stuff was wickedly expensive and not something they could grow on-site.

As he began to think about everything he needed to

explain to Emily, he felt his stomach tense up a little. There was a lot to managing even a small farm like Goosefeather. Stepping in cold turkey would have been a challenge for anybody, but for a city girl like Emily, it was going to be next door to impossible. Unless she was willing to accept his help, she was never going to meet the county extension agent's standards for animal and crop care.

And then there was the whole business about her plans to sell the farm. He'd expected that, but hearing her say it out loud had set him back a pace or two.

He sighed, hoping Emily had the sense to put on a pot of coffee after she finished straining the milk. When it came to talking and explanations, he was every bit as far out of his comfort zone as Emily was out here dealing with Beulah.

He had a feeling this might take a while.

Chapter Three

Emily set the brimming pail carefully on the side of the old-fashioned apron sink and removed its loose lid. Phoebe's egg had actually made it intact into the carton in the refrigerator, so Emily was able to get straight to straining the milk.

"Go wash your hands," she instructed the twins, "and use plenty of soap." Taking her own advice, Emily turned on the hot water faucet and squirted a generous dose of dishwashing liquid onto her hands. When she finished, she twisted the old-fashioned faucet off firmly. It had always dripped if you didn't wrench it down tightly.

She was struck again by how little had changed on Goosefeather Farm. The fading afternoon sun still filtered through the same red-checkered curtains, and there were still terra-cotta pots of blooming geraniums lining the bookshelf under the wide kitchen window. The walls were the same creamy yellow, and the old wooden floor was showing its familiar signs of wear around the doorways and in front of the sink and the enormous freestanding stove.

This kitchen had been Emily's happy place on the farm. There was something about this airy room that had always made her itch to pull out her grandmother's ceramic mixing bowls, get the heavy crocks of flour down out of the huge pantry and bake something crumbly and sweet.

As she dealt with the milk, she reconsidered the space with a more experienced eye. The fixtures and the appliances needed updating badly, but the kitchen had a great flow and boasted some amazingly generous work surfaces. This room had been designed for serious cooking and canning, unlike the cramped kitchen she and Clary made do with in their Atlanta apartment. With just a smidgen of updating, this could be the kitchen of her dreams. If it were located somewhere else.

Anywhere else.

Emily finished straining the milk through the dairy filter into clean half-gallon glass jars and set it to cool in an ice-water bath, a task she'd done twice a day during the summers she'd spent here. Inside work had always played to Emily's strengths, and since Sadie Elliott had never liked to spend any more time indoors than she had to, they had worked it out between them.

That was the one thing that had changed on Goosefeather Farm, Emily reflected sadly. Her grandfather Elliott had died before she was old enough to remember him, but her grandmother had been such a part of this place that it was almost impossible to believe she was gone. Emily half expected to see the old lady thumping down the kitchen stairs with her gardening hat on, heading out to wage war against the summer weeds. Emily blinked back her tears resolutely and lifted her chin.

She wouldn't go there.

It'd be selfish to wish her grandmother back. For the past few years, Grandma had made no secret of the fact that she was ready, as she put it, "to get on to the next thing." Once she'd reached her eighties, she said that the good Lord had tarried long enough.

Emily was thankful that her grandmother's earthly journey had ended peacefully, but Sadie Elliott had sure left a big hole behind her. Emily sighed. Then she firmed up her lips, squared her shoulders and got busy. She had enough sorrow under her belt to know that the best way to fill up this kind of empty spot was with hard work.

There were some benefits to growing up with a mother whose idea of a meal was nuking a frozen waffle in the microwave and who couldn't have cared less what kind of mess her daughter made in the kitchen. Emily had started cooking as soon as she was big enough to reach the oven controls, and she'd spent the last few years baking and waitressing in the hectic environment of a busy coffee shop. She might be clueless about managing a farm, but she knew her way around a kitchen. By the time Abel came through the back door, she had the coffee dripping fragrantly into its carafe and her children eating snacks in front of Grandma's ancient television.

"Animals are all settled for the evening," he said, crossing to the sink and beginning to lather up his hands. Emily noticed that he left the dishwashing liquid alone in favor of the little orange-colored bar of homemade soap in its dish.

"I sure wish we were," Emily muttered under her breath. She had the three-hour trip back to Atlanta in front of her, and the twins were already exhausted. It wasn't going to be a fun drive.

And there was still this conversation with Abel to get through. She might as well get that over with. "Have a seat," she invited. "I'll pour the coffee."

"I was hoping you'd think to make some." Abel pulled out a chair at the immense table that filled the center of the kitchen and slid his long legs under its checkered cloth.

"I don't know about you, but I think it's necessary." She poured two mugs, black. She remembered that Abel had never doctored his coffee with cream or sugar, and she'd had to learn to drink hers plain because black coffee was cheaper. "It's been a long day, and if I'm going to stay awake for the drive back, I'm going to need all the help I can get."

Abel nodded. "I'm sure you're ready to get on the road. I won't stay long, but I thought your mind might rest easier if we went ahead and got a few things settled between us." He accepted the cherry-red mug of coffee, flashing his crooked smile at her in thanks.

"You're probably right." She wasn't looking forward to it. She hated negotiations when she was the one needing favors. The incident with the rooster had really scared her, though. It would be too easy for the twins to get hurt on the farm. She was going to have to keep one eye on them all the time, and that meant she had to have some help. Stalling, Emily turned to the counter and opened a green-striped bakery box. "I hope you like muffins."

"I like pretty much anything I don't have to cook, but you don't have to feed me. The coffee's plenty."

"I brought these from the coffee shop where I work.

It's not any trouble to share them." Emily took down two of her grandmother's thick white plates and set an oversize muffin on each one. Casting a quick look back at the tall man sitting at the table, she considered, and then added a second muffin to one of the plates. Abel Whitlock had always been lean, but if her memory served, he had a hearty appetite.

"Thanks." Abel picked up one of the muffins and toyed briefly with the thin silver paper on its bottom before setting it back down on the plate. "These look real good, but I can't eat your food, Emily, until I'm sure you understand where I stand on this. I know you're finding it hard to believe, but I'm on your side here. I want to help you."

"Even though you'll get the farm if I don't stick this out?" She offered him a wry smile, but this time his expression remained serious.

"This farm is yours by rights. Miss Sadie was your family, not mine, and I'm sorry she left things like she did. I truly am."

He sounded sincere, and Emily felt a niggle of guilt. Abel had no family worth speaking of. His mother had run off when Abel was just a boy, leaving him to deal with his younger brother and their moody, alcoholic father as best he could.

Her grandmother had told her about the morning Abel had knocked on the farmhouse door. A fourteen-year-old boy with hungry eyes, he'd asked if he could split firewood for her in exchange for some food for himself and his little brother.

"I almost ran him off the property," Grandma had told Emily, shaking her head ruefully. "I'd been living next to the Whitlocks for too long not to be suspicious of them. Most of them would steal anything that wasn't nailed down. But he was nothing but a boy, skinny as a beanpole and so famished he was shaking. No telling when he'd eaten last. Elton Whitlock never cared much about anything that didn't come straight out of a liquor bottle, and he sure wasn't troubling his sorry head about feeding those boys of his after Gina left him. But that young'un had more gumption in his little finger than the rest of his kin put together. He wouldn't even eat the sandwich I brought out to him unless I let him earn it. So in the end I just handed him the ax and let him get on with it."

At the end of that day, Sadie Elliott had a neatly stacked woodpile that would last her for a month of cold weather, and young Abel had gone home with a new shirt on his back, a basket stuffed with eggs and vegetables from her garden and a job on Goosefeather Farm for as long as he wanted it. Abel had been family to Sadie ever since that day, and Emily knew it.

She got very busy peeling the paper off a muffin before she spoke. "You don't have to apologize for meaning a lot to my grandmother, Abel. And I don't blame you for the way she left her will. You and I both know nobody could talk Grandma into doing anything she didn't want to do."

Abel heaved a deep sigh, and she looked up from her muffin to find him smiling that lopsided smile of his. He looked relieved. "That's good to hear." He stripped the paper off one of his own muffins and broke off a generous chunk.

"That doesn't mean I'm happy about being put through this trial by farm, or whatever you want to call it," Emily cautioned. "It's the craziest thing I ever heard of. I don't know what Grandma was thinking."

"The letter didn't tell you?"

Emily shrugged. "Grandma never thought I appreciated Goosefeather Farm the way she wanted me to. It looks like she just wanted one last opportunity to change my mind. She was always convinced I belonged here."

"Maybe you do," Abel said simply, breaking off another chunk of muffin.

"Believe me, I don't." He looked as unconvinced as her grandmother had every time they'd had this particular conversation. Time to change the subject. "How are those muffins? I baked them yesterday morning." She was tinkering with her apple spice muffin recipe, and she thought adding the extra ground cloves had been a good idea.

"Really good. But then you always were a good cook, even when you were a little slip of a thing. Better than Miss Sadie, rest her soul. Her muffins were like hockey pucks."

Emily smiled, remembering. "She mixed them too much. You've got to be careful with muffin batter. I always told her so, but you know Grandma. Whatever she did, she did with a vengeance."

Abel chuckled. "You're right about that. Miss Sadie never did do things by halves. I recall when she finally got fed up with my excuses about not going to church with her. She went out in the middle of a Saturday night and flattened her own truck tires, all four of them, so I'd have to come over and drive her into town. Then she made a big show of stumbling on the curb in front of the church so I'd be sure to walk her in. She had me sitting in that pew before I knew what had happened, and she was right beside me, grinning like a mule eating briars." He sighed. "I'm sure going to miss her."

Emily nodded and took a deliberate sip of her scalding coffee to dissolve the lump in her throat. "I know. Me, too."

She'd been right to give him two muffins. He polished them both off in short order. She watched as he carefully wiped up the few crumbs he'd dropped on the table and deposited them on the plate next to his neatly folded muffin papers. Then he drained his coffee mug, set it on the plate and rose to carry his dirty dishes to the sink.

Abel had always done that, she remembered. He'd cleaned up after himself, been careful to remove his muddy boots at the back door and never left one crumb or drop behind. It had seemed so strange for such a big, outdoorsy boy to be so meticulous about things like that that Emily had found it amusing. She'd joked about it one time to her grandmother, and Sadie Elliott's sharp reply had caught her off guard. "Them that's had their share of trouble know better than to make trouble for other folks, missy! Mark that, and remember it."

"Emily?"

She glanced up, startled to find Abel standing at the sink looking uneasy.

"Yes?" She tilted her head to look up at him, thinking that inside the house he seemed bigger somehow. He'd always been tall, but she never remembered him taking up so much *space* before.

"I reckon we've circled around all this long enough. I don't want to upset you, but I'm going to speak plain. You're going to lose this farm if you don't have good help. There's just no two ways about it, and I'd sure hate to see that happen."

He'd filled out, Emily realized suddenly. Abel couldn't be called lanky anymore. He was still lean, but his shoulders had broadened, and there was a muscular set to them now. When she'd left Goosefeather Farm six years ago, Abel Whitlock was only a few years out of his teens. Now he was a man. That was the difference she was picking up on.

She felt a sudden prickle of nerves. Maybe this deal with Abel wasn't such a good idea after all. Then again, she knew he made a good point. If she didn't have help, she'd never be able to keep this place afloat.

It looked like she was trapped between this rock of a man and a very hard place.

"Listen to me, Emily. I know you're not easy in your mind about any of this. You don't like leaning on somebody else, and I can't say as I blame you. I'd likely feel the same if I were in your shoes. But I'm no stranger to you. You've known me nearly half your life, and you surely know me well enough by now to know that I mean what I say. If you let me help you, I'll make sure you end up with this farm at the end of the summer. You have my word on it."

For a second, all Emily could do was blink at this man standing in her grandmother's kitchen in faded jeans and a threadbare shirt. Apparently he was so determined to forfeit a tidy little inheritance that he was promising his help to the very person who was going to do her best to make sure he didn't get it. Was it even possible that such a person still existed in this dog-eat-dog world?

"Come on, Emily," he coaxed, one side of his mouth

quirking up. "You must have one last Goosefeather Farm summer left in you." Suddenly there was something irresistible about that crooked smile. She found herself smiling right back at him, and that was when it happened.

Emily felt a quick, flooding warmth around her heart, and her stomach dropped abruptly out from under her as if she'd just unexpectedly barreled down the slope of a roller coaster. She froze while Abel calmly turned his attention to rinsing out his coffee cup at the sink.

What had just happened?

Her mind stuttered with the shock of it. Had she just had some kind of weak-kneed, girlie moment? Over *Abel Whitlock?*

Surely not.

She'd thought she was dealing really well with Grandma's death, all things considered, but she was obviously more overwrought than she'd realized. Because Emily Elliott didn't have weak-kneed, girlie moments over men anymore. She'd learned her lesson in that department a long time ago, and she had no plans to go down that particular road again any time soon—if ever.

And if and when she did, it certainly wouldn't be with another man from Pine Valley, Georgia.

Abel turned back from the sink to find Emily studying him with a wary expression on her face. As he watched, her cheeks flushed pink, and her gaze darted back into her coffee cup.

She was still acting skittish, but who could blame her after the day she'd had? Judging from those purple smudges under her eyes, she was tuckered out. He could hear the twins arguing in the living room, something about a cartoon. Emily still had to load them up and make the trip back to Atlanta tonight. Abel felt a flicker of doubt. As much as he wanted to get this all settled, maybe right now wasn't the best time. He hesitated, shifting his weight from one foot to the other and wishing he knew just what to say to put her mind at ease.

"Abel." Something in Emily's voice jerked his wandering thoughts to attention. Now she was sitting bolt upright in her chair, and she looked as taut as a newly strung fence wire.

His muscles tensed. Something was wrong. "What is it?"

She swallowed, and very, very slowly she scooted the old ladder-back chair a few inches backward. "I think…" she whispered. "Okay, I know it sounds a little crazy, but I think there might be something *alive* under this table."

Abel's mind flashed to the screened door, to how it had seemed to be open just a crack when he came up the back steps, and he winced. On Goosefeather Farm that could only mean one thing, and he didn't think Emily was going to like it one little bit.

Before he could gather his thoughts enough to speak, something gray and long snaked out from under the low-hanging tablecloth and jabbed Emily smartly on the thigh. She yelped, and the mug she'd been holding hit the floor and cracked into pieces, sending the remains of her coffee flooding across the floorboards. Emily tipped her chair over backward, her legs tangling up in its slats as she scrambled away.

She was halfway into the living room before she stopped to look back. "What is it?" she asked in a trembling voice as the creature sidled slowly out from under the table.

"She's an African gray goose." Abel tried to keep the laugh out of his voice, but he couldn't entirely manage it. "I gave her to Miss Sadie last spring because I figured any farm called Goosefeather ought to have at least one goose living on it. Your grandma named her Glory. And she's a born troublemaker." He addressed his last comment to the goose, who honked briefly at him in reply.

Emily stayed safely in the living room, her arms wrapped protectively around her twins. They'd left their cartoon to blink owlishly at the unrepentant goose, who was doing her best to thieve the remains of Emily's muffin off the top of the kitchen table. "Thanks, but you can skip over the introductions. I don't think I want to be on a first-name basis with that thing. How did it get in here?"

"You must have left the screen door cracked when you headed out to the barn earlier. She's smart about opening it if it's not pulled all the way shut. Your grandma thought it was a cute trick, and that didn't help."

Emily directed a hard stare at the bird. "She bit me."

"She does that. Your grandma spoiled her. She wants some of your muffin."

As if to prove his point, Glory twisted her long neck and finally managed to reach the rest of the muffin on Emily's plate. Knocking it to the floor, the goose devoured her spoils greedily. She nibbled at the crumbs, glanced cautiously up at Abel and then turned her sleek head to consider the trio of strangers standing in the living room doorway.

Whatever Glory saw must not have sat too well with her, because she let out a loud honk and took three waddling steps in their direction, stretching her gray wings out widely. Phoebe's face crumpled in fright, and she began to cry.

"Make it go away, Mama! It's going to bite me!"

"No, it's not." As he watched, Emily got hold of herself, tilted that chin of hers up and let go of her twins. "Don't be scared. It's only a goose, sweetie."

"But you ran away from it," Phoebe protested, burying her face in her mother's shirt. "And it bit you!"

"Just a little nip. It didn't even hurt."

"But you hollered. Loud." Phoebe wasn't buying it.

"She surprised me, that's all. I wasn't expecting her to be under the table. She's just a spoiled pet and nothing to be afraid of." Emily took a brave, uncertain step in Glory's direction. "Shoo!" she said, flapping her hands at the bird. "Scat!"

Glory refused to scat. Instead she took another step in Emily's direction, extended her neck to its full length and honked again. Phoebe's wailing ratcheted up another notch, and even the unflappable Paul looked nervous.

"Please, Mr. Abel, make it go away!" the boy urged. "It's scaring Phoebe and Mama. And me, a little."

Abel took a quick step forward, but Emily halted him with a gesture and a fierce look. "I can handle this, Abel. If we're going to live here all summer, we're all going to have to learn to deal with the animals. You can't do everything for us. It's all *right*, Phoebe. Stop howling." Emily sounded exasperated.

"I don't want to stay here for the whole summer! Bad birds live here! I want to go ho-oome." Abel might not be any expert on kids, but even he could tell Phoebe had just about reached her limits. Poor little thing—first the rooster and now this.

"Emily, why don't you let me—" he started, but Emily interrupted him firmly.

"*No*, thanks. I told you. I can handle this." She took four determined steps back into the kitchen, and she and Glory eyed each other warily.

Abel's gut tensed. He didn't much like the direction this was taking. Scared people scared animals, and scared animals did unpredictable things.

The goose hissed and scrabbled her webbed feet on the floor as Emily neared her. Abel had been around nervous farm birds often enough to know exactly what was going to happen about two seconds before it did. Glory squatted briefly and produced a very large mess that splatted on the kitchen floor.

"It pooped!" To Abel's astonishment, Phoebe's wails abruptly turned into helpless giggles. "It pooped on the *floor*, Mama!"

"That's disgusting," Paul said quietly, but Abel saw a little smile sneaking around the corners of the boy's mouth.

Abel blinked and readjusted his thinking. All right. Maybe this was good. If the kids found this entertaining, they were going to love living on a farm. Poop, as they called it, was one thing there wasn't any shortage of.

"It's disgusting all right." Emily wasn't smiling, and Abel felt a little sorry for her. She handled those twins of hers like she'd been born a mother, but she clearly didn't know much about dealing with animals. "That bird's going outside right now."

"Emily," he tried again.

Emily was having none of it. "I told you, I've *got* this, Abel. Now, come on, bird. Glory. Whatever your name is. I think you've done enough damage for one day." Edging past the suspicious goose, Emily snagged another muffin out of the bakery box on the counter and positioned herself by the back door. "Let's get you outside where you belong." She broke off a piece of muffin and dropped it in a strategic spot halfway between the goose and the door to the back porch.

Glory angled her head and considered the offering with one beady brown eye before waddling over and gobbling it up. Emily tossed a second chunk of muffin a little closer to the doorway. Glory had caught on, and she immediately ambled over and ate that piece, too.

Emily turned to smile triumphantly at her children. "See? There's nothing to get upset about. You just have to stay calm around animals. If you use your brain, you can always figure out a way to outsmart them."

Something in Paul's expression tipped Abel off. He looked back at Emily just a fraction of a second too late to warn her that Glory had gotten impatient waiting for the next installment of muffin and was gearing up to nip Emily again, this time right on the seat of her jeans.

The chaos that followed left downy feathers floating airily around the kitchen and spilled coffee all over the floor. He was dimly aware of Emily's protests over the screaming twins, but this had gone far enough. Abel finally cornered the goose by the stove, and soon Glory was honking angrily on the back step.

Abel banged the screen door fully shut in the goose's face and went back into the house. Emily was already kneeling on the floor, wiping up the mess with the rags

Miss Sadie had kept in a bucket under her sink, two bright red spots burning high on her pale cheekbones.

She glanced up at Abel angrily. "I really wish you'd have let me deal with that."

He blinked. Now she was mad at him for getting the goose out of the kitchen? "Glory can be hard to manage. I was just trying to give you a hand."

"Well, next time I'd appreciate it if you'd wait until I ask you to help me." She splashed a rag into the bucket of soapy water with more force than necessary and scrubbed hard at the floor for a minute before looking back up at him. "I need you to understand something, Abel. I'm used to taking care of myself and my kids. I'm the one in charge of things, and I like it that way. I appreciate your offer to help me out. I really do, but when I say I want to handle something myself, I mean it."

He blew out a slow breath. Okay. This was about more than just the goose. He got that, but Emily wasn't the only one who was just about fed up. "Maybe you'd better write me up a handbook and let me study some, because apparently you've got a whole lot of rules about how you want to be treated that I don't know about." *And that don't make a lick of sense.* He left that part unsaid, which was good, because from the thunderous look on Emily's face he'd already said too much.

"You know, Abel, I don't think this is going to work out. I appreciate your offer, but I don't think it's a good idea."

"Aw now, Emily. You're overreacting. All I did—" he started out patiently, but Emily cut him off.

"All you did was push yourself in and take charge of a problem that was mine to deal with." She scrubbed at the floor viciously. "Twice. Once with the milking and the chores outside, and now this. Grandma was old, and she needed you to run things around here for her. I get that, but there's no need for us to have the same arrangement."

"Emily..."

"I'm done talking about this." She finished cleaning the floor and chunked the dirty rag into the bucket. "If you still want to be helpful, then take care of the animals tomorrow morning while I get arrangements made in Atlanta and write me up a list of instructions so that I can take over starting tomorrow evening. I'd really appreciate that."

"But—" he began patiently.

"But nothing. That's the way I want it, and this is my call." She spoke sharply, then glanced sideways at her staring children and composed herself. "I don't mean to be rude, Abel, I really don't. Please don't take it personally. I've just learned that I keep my balance a whole lot better when I stand on my own two feet. You start leaning on other people, and it's just a matter of time until you fall over."

"I think that kind of depends on who you're leaning on," Abel observed quietly.

Emily ignored him. She got up, set the tin bucket full of dirty rags on the back porch and began scrubbing her hands at the sink. "I'm going to give this floor a quick once-over with a mop and some disinfectant, and then I'm going to have to load up and go home. The lawyer said that was all right as long as I'm back here tomorrow." She sighed, blowing a stray tendril of curling hair off her flushed forehead. "Like I said, if you really want to help me, Abel, I'd appreciate it if you'd take care of the animals in the morning and leave me those written instructions so I'll know what to do when I get back tomorrow night."

"I'll be glad to take care of the animals for you. But—"

"Thanks. I appreciate it. Now, if you don't mind, it's been a hard day. I've got a lot to do and a long drive to make. I think we need to call this a night."

Well, she couldn't make herself any clearer than that. He nodded, forced a smile for the stunned-looking twins still standing in the living room doorway and walked outside.

He sat on the back stoop pulling on his boots while the insulted goose tugged spitefully at his shirtsleeve. He lingered there for an extra minute looking out over the pastures. The sun was dipping behind the ridge to the west of the farm, throwing red and gold streaks through the clouds. Unseen insects chirred peaceably in the grass around him, and he could smell the tang of the spearmint that always grew best in the moist shade by the porch. Miss Sadie had said that spearmint was worse than a weed the way it took over a place, and she was always threatening to root it up. But Abel liked a sprig of it in his iced tea, and he loved the fresh, sharp smell of it, weed or not.

Truth was, he loved every weed and stump on this old place. He'd told Miss Sadie once that he couldn't have loved Goosefeather Farm any more if he'd been born on it, and she'd chuckled and tousled his hair roughly. "Found God here, didn't you, sonny? So maybe you *were* born here in a way."

He heard the slap of Emily's mop against the old floor, and he felt a twinge of guilt. Maybe he'd had more to do with this whole mess than he'd thought. Maybe he shouldn't have let on to Miss Sadie how much the farm meant to him. Maybe that was why she'd left her will the way she had. It would figure. Every time he opened his mouth, he seemed bound to stick his foot in it.

Abel took in a deep, slow breath of evening air and squinted heavenward.

"Lord, I need Your help. I had some ideas about how to set this to rights, but it looks like I'm only making things worse, so I'm putting it in Your hands. You're the only one who can unscramble these eggs and get all this straightened out like it should be. Help me to do my part, and help me to have enough sense not to get in Your way. Amen."

There. He'd done all he could do for tonight.

Abel blew out one last sigh, gave Glory's silky head a stroke with a gentle fingertip and levered himself up off the chilly step to start the walk back to his cabin. He'd left Goosefeather Farm a thousand evenings before this one, but somehow tonight it felt different.

This time it felt kind of permanent.

Chapter Four

Emily stopped and pulled the crumpled square of notebook paper out of her back pocket, angling it to catch the beam of sunlight coming through the high barn window. She squinted at Abel's handwritten instructions in the fading afternoon light and sighed. The goats were the next thing on the list, but unfortunately they weren't the last. There was still an awful lot left to do, and it was getting dark fast.

The milking had taken longer than she'd expected. Her hand muscles were sorely out of shape, and she'd had to stop several times to flex her cramping fingers. She'd done her best, but she was pretty sure she hadn't stripped out Beulah's udder nearly as well as she should have.

At least she didn't have to worry about getting tonight's milk strained. Beulah had finally lost the last shred of her patience and kicked the bucket over. Emily knew she should be upset about the waste of that hard-earned milk, but instead she was just thankful she could cross another job off the evening's list.

And now she'd better get started mixing the goat

food. Judging from the number of ingredients Abel had put down, that was going to take her a while, too.

"Hello? Anybody home?" a female voice called from the barnyard. Emily tiptoed to look out the window and saw a trim brunette dressed in jeans and a green T-shirt standing on the gravel driveway beside a glossy red pickup truck. The woman glanced in Emily's direction and gave a quick wave before letting herself into the pasture. She latched the gate deftly behind herself and headed toward the barn, her gait easy and relaxed.

Emily glanced down at her filthy clothes and winced. Great. Company. Just what she didn't need right now.

The young woman came through the open barn doorway and stopped. "Well," she said, amusement rippling through her throaty voice. "You look like you've been working hard." She flashed a brilliant smile, revealing a deep dimple in each cheek. "I thought for once Pine Valley gossip had to have it all wrong, but here you are. Emily Elliott, as I live and breathe! It's been a long time."

Emily narrowed her eyes, searching her memory. The voice was familiar, but…

"Now, don't tell me you don't remember me." The girl raised her eyebrows until they nearly disappeared under the red ball cap she was wearing, her long dark ponytail threaded through the gap at the back. "Here. Let me help you out." She made circles with her thumbs and forefingers and placed them in front of her eyes like spectacles, stuck her front teeth over her bottom lip, and pooched out her slim stomach.

"Bailey Quinn!" Emily gasped. She laughed and rushed forward.

Bailey took a step backward and held her hands up as

a barrier. "Whoa there! Not until you've had a bath! Oh, never mind." She shook her head, took four quick steps forward and gave Emily a fierce, hard hug. "What's a little crud between old friends?"

"Bailey! I can't believe it! What are you doing here? I didn't even know you were still in Pine Valley. You always said…" Emily trailed off, unsure how to continue.

"We *both* always said," Bailey pointed out drily. "But here we are. You're standing in a barn covered with muck, and I'm peddling vegetables and homemade jams at the farmers' market and heading up the local 4-H chapter. Looks like country life got us both in the end."

"Looks like," Emily echoed faintly, her disbelieving eyes trying to make sense of Bailey's transformation. She couldn't get over how different her friend looked without the big, round spectacles she'd always worn, and with her teeth as straight and white as they could be. Then there was the little matter of her figure. "I can't believe…you're just… Wow. Just, wow! You look wonderful!"

"I ought to. Contacts," Bailey explained succinctly. "And braces. Five years of those awful things." She patted her flat stomach. "And a whole lot of carrot sticks and crunches."

Emily felt a surge of admiration. Her old friend might not have made it out of Pine Valley, but she had changed her life just the same. The mousy bookworm had turned into a dark-haired beauty.

"We need to catch up," Bailey was saying. "But from the look of you, now's obviously not the time. I just stopped by to drop off your check and take a peep at the garden and see what's coming off for Saturday. Looks like green beans, squash and a ton of tomatoes and peppers as near as I can tell. Time to crank out a batch of my signature spaghetti sauce." She pulled a folded check out of her pocket and wiggled it in Emily's direction. When Emily just looked at it, Bailey frowned and tilted her head. "Abel didn't tell you?"

"Tell me what?"

Bailey snorted. "That man! He'd rather take a jab in the eye with a stick than talk to a person. Your grandma and I had a deal. I've got a little specialty store downtown, Bailey's, and I run a booth at the farmers' market every Saturday. I sold Miss Sadie's vegetables for her, and in return she let me have half of them for the preserves and sauces I'm making for the store. I was hoping it'd suit you to keep the deal going." Bailey's straight teeth flashed in a quick smile. "Abel Whitlock isn't much of a talker, but everybody knows his vegetables are the best in town. My booth is mobbed every week." She fluttered the check. "Here. Take it. That's from the last few weeks, so don't get your hopes up that it'll be this much every time."

Emily reached out slowly and took the check. "You're running a store? Here?"

"Here, there and everywhere, honey. The internet is a marvelous thing. I'm just getting started, but so far so good. How about it?" Bailey tilted her head. "You want to let the deal stand?"

Emily blinked and tried to think fast. She wished Abel had told her about this. She hated having to make spur-of-the-moment decisions, but if Grandma had thought this arrangement with Bailey was a good idea for the farm, it probably was. "Sure. I guess so."

"Great!" Bailey's face lit up.

"I'm only here for the summer, though," Emily cautioned quickly. "My grandmother's will—"

"Oh, I know all about that," Bailey interrupted with a dismissive wave. "That will is the talk of the town." She chuckled and shook her head again, her ponytail swinging widely. "Lois Gordon is beside herself."

"I bet she is." A tiny smile tickled around the corner of Emily's lips as she imagined the scene that had ensued when Trey's mother heard Emily was staying in Pine Valley for three months.

"Yeah." Bailey's smile faded, and she looked at Emily soberly. A short silence, crowded with the events that had unfolded since the two friends last saw each other, stretched between them. "Be careful there, Emily. Mrs. Gordon's kind of a loose cannon these days. Ever since Trey… Since she heard you were back, she's been…" Bailey gave up and shook her head. "Just be careful."

Emily shrugged. "Lois Gordon's already done all the damage she can do to me, Bailey."

"Maybe so. I mean, if you really do plan on selling the farm and leaving town come fall." Bailey's dimples flashed again. "Got somebody waiting for you back in Atlanta?"

"Just a job," Emily replied, hoping she was telling the truth. "I'm too busy for anything else."

"That so? Then who knows? Abel might convince you to stick around here. He always was kind of sweet on you. You two will be spending so much time together out here, you never can tell. Some sparks might start flying." Emily's old friend's eyes twinkled mischievously.

Emily shook her head. "That's crazy. Abel and I are just friends." Her mind skipped to that inexplicable moment she'd had in the kitchen, but she dismissed it firmly. That had been nothing but exhaustion. "You're crazy," she repeated.

"Yeah," Bailey scoffed. "*I'm* crazy. Abel loves this place beyond all reason, always has. Folks in town thought he'd be happy as a clam to have a shot at having it for himself. Some thought maybe he'd even conned your grandma into leaving things the way she did. I mean—" Bailey shrugged eloquently "—people hear the name Whitlock, and that kind of thing comes to mind. But word is, he pestered the living daylights out of Jim Monroe trying to find a way for you to get the farm outright. Now, why do you figure he'd want to do something like that?"

"He's a nice guy."

"Nobody's that nice. Although I'll admit, Abel comes awfully close. You could go a lot farther and fare a lot worse, as the old folks say. Well, I'd better be getting on so you can finish up out here. Daylight's burning off fast. Come by the store sometime soon, and we'll have lunch. And be sure to bring those two cute kids I saw out there playing with the hose. I want to meet them. When they're not dripping wet, I mean. And, Emily? Welcome back." Bailey gave her one last perfect grin and sauntered back out toward the red pickup, waving cheerfully at the twins, who were headed to the barn.

"We filled up the cows' water trough and turned off the water," Paul announced as the twins came through the doorway. Bailey was right. They were both soaked.

"Are we all done yet? I'm tired." Phoebe dropped herself down on a hay bale and rested her chin on her hands. Emily opened her mouth to protest. The hay chaff would stick to the little girl's clothes and make a mess in the washing machine. She caught herself just in time and swallowed her words.

Keep things positive, she reminded herself.

"I know you're tired, hon, but we're making great progress!" And they were…for a city girl and two five-year-olds. "Now we get to go feed the goats! That'll be fun!"

Phoebe sighed heavily. "Nothing's fun here. It's all just work and dirt."

Out of the mouth of babes. Emily had felt just that way every single summer she'd spent at Goosefeather Farm. She mustered up an enthusiasm she was far from feeling and smiled widely. "You haven't seen the goats yet, sweetie! They're really smart animals, and they love to play. You'll like them."

"I seriously doubt it." Paul spoke matter-of-factly from his side of the hay bale. "We haven't liked anything so far."

Emily gave up and began scooping the goat pellets into a plastic bucket. She seriously doubted it, too. *Lord, please help us*, she prayed. *Let the twins find something they enjoy here. I hate to see them unhappy, but I don't know what to do to fix it.*

Emily checked Abel's instructions again and added another scoop of food. Even preparing the goat food was more involved than she'd imagined. She measured out some brown powder from the bucket marked Goat Minerals and sprinkled it over the bucket. Then she tossed in a handful of black sunflower seeds, a sprinkle of baking soda and a couple of teaspoons full of a probiotic powder. This was more complicated than mixing up a batch of muffins in the kitchen at Café Cup.

Which brought up another stressful point. Mr. Alvarez had been extremely displeased to discover that she was going to have to take so much time off work. He'd made it clear that Emily shouldn't expect him to hold her job until the autumn. If he had a vacancy, maybe she could come back to work, but he was making no promises.

The possibility that she was going to find herself jobless in Atlanta again had shadowed her thoughts all day. That had been one of the toughest times in her life. She still remembered the feelings of desperation and hopelessness.

But God had met her during those dark days. Emily reminded herself of that as she plunked the pail of food and several flakes of hay into a battered child's wagon that had been in use at Goosefeather Farm for as long she could remember. And God wouldn't let her down now.

"Come on, guys. Let's go feed the goats!" Emily forced enthusiasm into her voice, but the twins still groaned before getting to their feet.

"Come on, Pheebs. We might as well get this over with," Paul said gloomily.

Pulling the heavy wagon along the bumpy red clay path was harder than Emily remembered, and the twins were dragging their feet. The shadows were lengthening quickly as they walked down to the goat pasture, and Emily was glad she'd thought to snag the plastic flashlight from its shelf beside the barn door. She switched it on, and it reluctantly sputtered a little circle of dim light ahead of her. Uh-oh. She shook it, and the light flickered on and off. At least it was sort of working. It probably needed new batteries, but hopefully it'd hold out long enough to see them back to the farmhouse.

"Hear that noise?" she called cheerfully to the twins, who were trudging behind the wagon. "That's the tree frogs down by the creek! There must be hundreds of them this year!" Her observation met with a stony silence.

As they started down the last hill, a new sound broke through the twilight, and Emily stopped short, listening. The wagon she'd been pulling continued down the slope and banged sharply into the back of her calves. It hurt, and she felt frustration rising in her like a wave. She was dirty, sticky, hot and tired, and all she wanted to do was take a bath and collapse into bed. She did not need a weird noise right now.

"Mama, that frog sounds sick," Paul said worriedly. "And big."

"That's not a frog, Paul. I think it's a goat." And unless she missed her guess, it was an extremely unhappy goat. Something was wrong. She left the wagon where it was and sprinted the last few yards to the goat pasture.

In the dimming light she could make out the figures of several goats standing outside their little barn. Nothing seemed to be wrong with any of them, but they were intently focused on the dark doorway to the shed.

She soon found out why. From its depths came a guttural cry that made the hairs prickle up on the back of her neck.

Okay, there was a goat in there, and something was definitely wrong with it. The shed looked dark and spidery and generally icky, but she was going to have to go in there and try to deal with whatever the problem was. That's what responsible farmers did.

She *really* hated farming.

"Stay right here by the fence, you two," she told

the twins. "I'm going to check on the goat, and I'll be right back."

"But I don't want to stay out here in the da-ark," Phoebe sobbed.

Paul and Emily sighed in unison. Phoebe had probably cried more in the last twenty-four hours than she had in the last twenty-four days. Phoebe didn't handle change or stress very well. She never had. Emily was trying her best to be patient and supportive, but she had to admit that she was a little off her game at the moment.

The truth was, Emily didn't handle change or stress all that well, either.

"Give me your hand, Pheebs," Paul was saying. "I'll hold it until Mama comes back out."

Her sweet son was saving her bacon yet again. "Thanks, hon. I'll try not to be long."

Swallowing hard, Emily picked up a flake of the hay from the wagon and tossed it over the fence to distract the other goats. Then she went through the gate, shaking the little flashlight and willing it to light.

It flickered on, and she pointed it into the doorway of the shed. It illuminated the eyes of a bloated-looking goat lying on its side in the hay, and the animal promptly bellowed and started struggling to get up.

"Switch that off. You're spooking her. They're not used to artificial lights, and it's best not to use them until you have to." A masculine voice spoke from the corner of the dark shed, making Emily jump and drop the flashlight.

The impact caused the light to brighten, and the goat cried out again and thrashed her legs. Abel reached out from the shadows and grabbed the offending object. He switched it off, and the shed was plunged back into darkness.

For a few heart-pounding seconds, Emily could see nothing at all. Then as her eyes adjusted, she made out Abel leaning against one corner of the murky little building, his long legs stretched out in front of him.

"What are you doing here?" she asked.

"Waiting."

She swallowed. "Waiting for what?"

"You, for one thing. You're running a little late with the goat feed, aren't you?"

Emily felt her hackles rising. "Sorry. I didn't figure the goats had any place to be."

"Animals need to eat on a schedule. It stresses them out if they're late getting fed."

Another thing she was doing wrong. Fine. He could add it to the list. The goat made another loud cry, and Emily's heart sank guiltily. "Is that what's wrong with her? Seriously? She's like that because I was an hour late feeding her?"

Abel's chuckle drifted through the darkness. "No. Cherry's the other thing I'm waiting on. I've been watching her for the past week, and I figured it was about her time, so I came by to check. She's going to kid."

The goat was in labor. Well, that explained it. Emily cast her mind back to her summers at Goosefeather Farm, trying to remember what she could about the kidding process. Since goats usually had their babies in early spring, Emily had only seen a couple of births.

She did notice one strange thing about this one. "Why's she lying down? I thought goats usually gave birth standing up."

"Most do. But Cherry's an older goat, and she tends to have some problems. That's why I've been keeping an eye on her. When I saw her this morning, I figured she was getting close. I've come over and checked on her a couple times."

"But you didn't mention it to me."

She heard Abel shifting in the crackling straw. "No. I didn't."

Her nervousness and exhaustion solidified into annoyance. He was elbowing her aside again, just like he'd done in the barn and in the farmhouse kitchen. How could she take care of things she didn't even know about? "You should have written me a note about this goat, and I could have checked on her myself. And Bailey Quinn stopped by with a check and a long story about a deal she had with Grandma. I'd have appreciated a heads-up on that, too."

The goat made another loud noise, which was echoed outside by a sob from Phoebe.

"Mama, I'm scared!"

"It's okay, sweetie!" Emily called out cheerfully. "Mr. Abel's here, and the goat's about to have a little baby!"

Abel shifted again in the corner, and suddenly a steady beam of light illuminated the shed. That figured. His flashlight was bigger than hers. And it worked.

"I thought you said no lights," Emily said crabbily, and then felt a twinge of embarrassment. She sounded as whiny as Phoebe.

"Nope. I said it was best not to use them until you had to. Now we have to." Abel carefully heaped up some straw, propping up the flashlight so that it shone on the goat's backside, where Emily could see a dark bubble protruding. Her heartbeat quickened as the goat made another pained noise, but Abel seemed completely calm. "Things are moving along fine. Why don't you get the twins in here? I doubt they've seen anything like this before."

"You underestimate the powers of YouTube," she replied drily, but she stuck her head out of the barn and called the children in. They came reluctantly, still holding hands, and their eyes widened at the scene that greeted them.

"Is that goat dying?" Paul asked solemnly.

"No," Emily reassured him. "Like I said, it's the other way round. She's about to have a baby."

"That's messy," Phoebe pronounced, wrinkling her nose.

"Well, I can't argue with you there," Abel said. "But lots of things that start out messy end up pretty good if you just hang in there. Watch and see."

Emily half expected her daughter to refuse, but instead the little girl dropped her brother's hand and crept over to Abel's side. "Is that the baby?" she asked, pointing to the enlarging bubble.

"No, the baby's inside that sac. In a minute or two we should see hooves. They come first, then the nose."

Phoebe mimicked Abel's position, crouching down beside him to peer intently at the goat's backside. The little girl was concentrating so hard that she leaned a little too far forward. She swayed precariously, and Abel put out an instinctive hand to steady her, his eyes never straying from the laboring goat. The little girl took hold of his muscled arm and held on, balancing herself.

Emily felt a warm pressure gently squeeze her heart. As annoying as Abel Whitlock could be, she had to admit he was good with the twins, even Phoebe, who wasn't an easy child to charm.

There was something rocklike about the man, a steadiness that seemed somehow quiet and safe and immovable. It was also frustrating if you happened to be the woman beating your head against it. A phrase from her grandmother's letter flitted through her mind. *Harder to move than a sack of bees.*

"See?" Abel was saying. "Here he comes."

Tiny yellowish hooves were now visible, and they could see a little brown snout resting peacefully on top of them.

"He looks like he's praying," Paul said, edging closer.

"If he isn't he should be," Abel answered with a chuckle. "This is a pretty important day for him."

Emily watched guiltily as the big man spread a handful of clean straw over the birth area. She knew she should be in there handling all this, but she was so tired. If she had to navigate one more learning curve today, there was a very real possibility that she might start screaming and never stop.

She backed up a step and sagged against the planks of the shed wall, past caring about the dirt and potential spiders. Abel wanted to do this. Fine. She'd let him handle it, and hopefully she'd live to fight another long, dirty and exhausting day.

Abel's attention was focused on the laboring goat, but he was dimly aware that Emily had removed herself to a corner of the shed. She'd apparently decided to give in and let him deal with the birth without a fuss. That was a relief.

Cherry gave a strain, and suddenly the baby goat,

still enclosed in his birth sac, slid out onto the clean straw. Abel sprang into action, quickly releasing the kid from the membrane and rubbing him hard with a towel he pulled from a sack in the corner. He flipped the bleating baby over and clamped the umbilical cord with a tiny plastic clamp. Sure enough, it was a little buck. He'd guessed as much when he'd first seen the baby's blocky head.

"Here." He wrapped the wet kid in the towel and pushed him toward Phoebe. "Hold him still, sweetheart. I've got to put some medicine on him."

He'd already figured out that Phoebe was the more squeamish of the two, but she had something of her mother's grit. After only an instant's hesitation, she put her hands gently around the slimy baby. "Why does he need medicine? Is he sick?"

"No, and we're going to keep it that way." Quickly Abel measured iodine into the cap of the bottle and doused the umbilical stump with it. "All done now." He gave the baby another quick toweling and then leaned forward and settled him next to his mother. Cherry sniffed him appreciatively and made a little chuckling noise deep in her throat.

"She likes him!" Phoebe sounded jubilant.

"Of course she does, silly. All mothers love their babies."

Paul's innocent statement made Abel's heart tighten. He knew better, but he felt a rush of thankfulness that this solemn little boy didn't. He glanced up at Emily, who was standing with her arms crossed defensively just where the flashlight ebbed into dark.

He smiled at her, but her lips stayed stubbornly straight. She was still ticked.

"Well, looks like the show's over," Emily said briskly. "We'd better give the other goats their feed and get back to the house. We've still got chores to finish, and as Mr. Abel pointed out, we're running late already."

That comment of his had really rankled with her. This was not just a woman who liked to do things for herself; she also wanted to get everything right the first time. It was too bad he had to point out her mistake.

"Oh, I don't think the show's over quite yet." Abel winked at Phoebe and Paul. "Goats generally have twins."

"Twins! That's our favorite thing!" Phoebe clapped her hands gleefully and hunkered back down into position as the goat made a guttural noise and strained again. "Come on, Cherry! You can do it!"

Abel's heart expanded about two sizes as he looked at the little girl's excited face in the soft glow of the flashlight. He'd dealt with plenty of animal births since he started working with Miss Sadie, with all kinds of outcomes, but he'd never shared one with a child before. Seeing it all unfold through Phoebe's and Paul's eyes made the experience brand-new for him, too.

This must be what it was like to be a father, he realized. You got to see all the little things in life with fresh eyes.

He glanced back at Emily. She caught his eye and tilted up that infuriating chin. "There's really no point in both of us staying. I can handle the rest of this."

His reprieve was over. This woman was as frustrating as shoveling mud. She pushed away help with both hands and planted her feet stubbornly right in the middle of trouble with a mixture of foolishness and bravado that worried his heart and stirred it all at the same time.

Yes, Emily Elliott was an unsettling woman, the kind of woman who could keep a man off balance for the rest of his life if he let her. He should be thankful she was only here for the summer.

Cherry shifted on the hay slightly and made an uncomfortable noise. It looked like that second twin was going to arrive pretty soon. Abel glanced from the goat to Emily's shadowed face, trying to feel out what to do. "I don't mind finishing up, and Cherry's used to me."

"She'll have to get used to me sooner or later, and there's no time like the present." Emily spoke lightly, but Abel could hear the steel beneath her words. "I really appreciate all your help, but I'll take it from here."

This wasn't a good idea, but he had a feeling that even if he won this battle, he'd end up losing the war for sure. He sighed. "Let me take the barn flashlight then, and you keep this one. You'll need a good light."

Emily made a noise as if she were going to argue, then stopped herself. "Thanks. I'll return yours as soon as I can."

He nodded, cast one last worried look at Cherry and walked slowly out the door of the barn into the cool freshness of the night. The goats were milling around outside the barn as they tended to do when one of them was birthing, and they nuzzled against him as he went by. Abel caressed their soft noses, feeling guilty. They trusted him, and here he was leaving one of them when she needed help. That didn't sit well with him at all. He went out the gate, banging it a little harder than he normally would.

His insides were twisting around like a net full of snakes, and he didn't like the feeling one bit. If something went sideways with the twin, and with Cherry that was about as likely as not, Emily wouldn't have a clue what to do. Abel stood in the path for a moment, torn.

He heard a babble of excited voices coming from the little barn, and he felt a punch of disappointment. The twin must have been born, and he'd missed it. Worse than that, he'd also been cheated out of seeing the twins experience it. Funny how hard you could take missing out on something you didn't even know about half an hour ago.

"Mr. Abel!" Paul came barreling through the gate. "Come quick! Something's wrong, and Mama doesn't know what to do!"

Abel sprinted back into the barn to find Emily crouched down behind Cherry. She glared at him as he knelt beside her.

"I told Paul not to call you back. I can manage."

Abel took one good look and shook his head. "Not this time. Like I said, Cherry tends to have problems. See that?" He pointed to where the second sac was bulging out.

"What?" Emily leaned farther into the circle of light. "It looks the same as the other one."

"Look again."

"No hooves," Paul said softly. "Just a nose this time. That's why I called Mr. Abel."

Emily leaned even closer. "You're right. Why didn't I see that?"

"Most people wouldn't have. You've got a good eye, son. The legs are doubled back. We'll have to pull them forward." He rummaged in the medical kit he'd left behind in the straw.

Phoebe was standing in a corner looking uneasy,

two fingers in her mouth. "Eww," she said softly, and
he turned back to see that the sac had ruptured.

Cherry was putting him through his paces this time.
"Okay. We're on the clock now," he said aloud. "This
baby needs to come into the world fast, or she'll suf-
focate."

"It's a girl?" Phoebe asked excitedly. "The twins are
going to be one boy and one girl like me and Paul,
Mama!"

"Sure looks like it," Abel said, grinning.

"You think so?" Emily sounded skeptical. "How can
you possibly tell at this point?"

"Well, I'm guessing, but that's a pretty slender little
nose there. I'd say we're looking at a doe this time."
He pulled a pair of plastic gloves over his hands and
squirted a lubricating gel on his fingers.

"What are you doing?" Phoebe had drawn closer
again.

"I'm going to pull her little legs forward so she can
be born," Abel answered. He carefully hooked his finger behind one of the forelegs at the shoulder and pulled
it gently forward until the tiny hoof was pointing in the
right direction.

"Yay!" Phoebe clapped. "That's one!"

"One to go." Abel fought a smile as he went after the
other leg. Phoebe clapped again and cheered when the
second little hoof was pointed outward.

Abel gave up and let the grin spread across his face.
He'd helped Cherry with several tricky births over the
years, but he'd never had a cheering section before. It
was kind of nice.

He could get used to it.

With the legs in the right position, the birth went fast,

and soon a little doe was nuzzling next to her brother. Cherry struggled to her feet, anxious to look her new babies over.

"Here." Abel handed Paul an empty feed pan. "Go out and put some feed in this dish for Cherry, and then you'd better pour the rest of the food in the trough outside for the others."

"Why don't you go and help him, Phoebe? Mr. Abel and I just need to clean up and then we'll head back to the house." Emily was already gathering up the supplies he'd strewn all over the straw and packing them neatly back into the medical kit.

"I'll wait here until Cherry passes the afterbirth," Abel said, "and then I'll head home myself."

Emily groaned. "I forgot about that part." She swiped her hair out of her face with one hand, leaving a generous smear of dirt on her forehead. She looked as wilted as a pretty little rag doll with only about half her stuffing in.

"You can take the twins and head back like you said. I'll wait. It can take an hour or two, and the little ones are tired out."

"I can't ask you to do that." Emily's voice was quiet, and he noticed that her hands were shaking as she picked up the bottle of iodine and placed it back in the bag. "You've already done more than you should have. I'll manage. Just tell me what to do."

Not this again. "You're not asking me. I'm offering. Don't be bullheaded, Emily. There's already been enough of that for one night."

She froze and tilted her head to glare up at him. "I'm not being bullheaded. I'm being responsible."

"That may be what you're calling it, but I don't think that's what it is."

"Really?" The chin tilted up another notch. "So, what would you call it, then?"

He waited a beat and then answered her quietly, "Fear. I think you're scared to death."

She stared at him, and he saw something shift in her expression. She went from looking about two inches away from blowing up to looking about two inches away from tears. Abel felt a tickle of uneasiness. All in all, he'd rather she blew up.

"Mama?" A worried voice spoke from the door, but neither of them looked in that direction. Their eyes were locked on each other.

"I'll be right there, Paul." Emily's voice cracked a little, and Abel felt guilty. She'd obviously had a tough day, and she was stressed and tired. He shouldn't make things worse.

"There are no strings attached here, Emily. This is nothing but an old friend offering you a hand. You might better take it."

"Mama?" Paul's voice sounded a little more urgent.

"Just a minute, Paul." Emily swallowed and looked down at her hands. "It's not that I don't appreciate the offer, Abel, but…"

"No more *buts* tonight." He offered her an encouraging smile. "Save those for tomorrow. Go on. Take your kids and put them in the bed. I'll handle the rest of this." He could see her wavering, which proved just how tired she really was.

"Mama!"

Emily made an exasperated noise. "Paul, you're interrupting. We're about to go home." She got stiffly to her feet, winced and gave in. "Mr. Abel is going to finish up with Cherry so that I can get you two in the bed."

"That's good, but, Mama?"

"What?"

"Before we go to bed, I think we're going to need some more flashlights."

Emily and Abel both frowned. "Why?" she asked her son suspiciously.

"Because Phoebe forgot to close the gate when we went to get the food. All the goats got out."

Chapter Five

"Is this where Mr. Abel lives?" Phoebe spoke from the backseat. "Wow!"

Emily parked the car and stared. Wow, indeed. She'd only been to Abel's home once, when her grandmother delivered some chicken soup because Abel was down with a bad summer cold. Abel's father had been living then, and Emily remembered the ramshackle log cabin looking stark and unkempt, surrounded by a generous litter of bottles and trash. She also remembered the tightness of her grandmother's lips as she'd maneuvered her pickup truck back down the slope of the mountain.

Things had changed.

Before, the small cabin had sat like a scab on the mountain, unattractive and out of place. Now it looked as if it had grown up naturally there, as much a part of the hillside as the pines that surrounded it. The yard was spotless, and a meandering path of flat stones led the way to the front porch, which sheltered a man-sized rocking chair and a small table. Just one chair, Emily noticed. Abel must not be much for company.

Sparkling new nine-paned windows had replaced the

cracked ones, and the round curve of the logs gleamed a warm golden brown in the dappled sunlight. As she opened the car door and stepped out, she could smell the tang of the dry pine needles under her feet and hear the birds trilling in the treetops. The cool air beneath the bristly pine canopy was heavy with peace.

Under Abel's care the Whitlock place had gone from being an eyesore to the kind of cabin city people spent big money to vacation in. Deep down Emily wasn't really surprised. Abel seemed to have a gift for coaxing calm out of chaos.

She took a fresh grip on the foil-covered plate she held in her hands and smiled at the twins, who had clambered out of the car to stand beside her. "All right, guys. Let's go have a talk with Mr. Abel."

Up on the lofty porch, she knocked on the dark green door and waited. Nothing happened.

"Maybe he's not here." Phoebe sounded disappointed. The prospect of seeing Abel had kept Emily's daughter bouncing happily in the backseat during the whole of the short drive over.

"His truck is here," Paul argued. "I saw it parked around back."

"Well, we'll go around back, then." Emily hoped Abel was home. She wasn't sure she could screw up her courage to do this a second time.

Behind the cabin they discovered another small log building, and Emily could faintly hear the strains of country music coming from it. This time their knock was answered.

Abel stood in the doorway, the front of his shirt dusted over with tiny tendrils of wood, a chisel in one hand. At the sight of them his expression warmed, his lips crooking upward in his easy, lopsided smile.

"Well, now! Look who's come to visit. I had a feeling this day was going to bring me something special."

"I hope we're not interrupting your work," Emily began before Phoebe broke in.

"Mama brought apple bread for you to say thank you for helping us with the goats last night. And I'm supposed to 'pologize for letting the goats get out. I already did, but Mama said to tell you again because you had to chase them for *hours*."

Abel flicked Phoebe's nose with a gentle finger. "It's all right, sweetheart. Gates are tricky things sometimes. I've left a few open myself, and so has your mama." His eyes twinkled over at Emily, reminding her silently of the many times he'd had to round up animals *she'd* accidently let out. She flushed, and Abel grinned. "So, apple bread? Is that what I smell?" His glance dropped down to the plate Emily held in her hands and then came back up to her face.

She nodded, hating the blush she felt brightening her cheeks. What was it about this man that made her act like a self-conscious schoolgirl? "I hope you like it."

"I'm sure I will. I've never had apple bread before, but it sounds like something that would go good with a cup of coffee."

"You've never had it before, because Mama just made it up this morning." Paul tilted his head to peer around Abel into the workshop. "She's all the time making up new recipes. Are you making something? Can we see?"

"Paul." Emily was mortified. "Mr. Abel's busy."

"Sure you can. Come on in."

Like the cabin, Abel's workshop was neat and bright, its walls studded with shelves of tools and carvings in various stages of completion. There were a lot of them, and the place had a professional air to it. Emily blinked. She hadn't realized that he took his carving so seriously.

"We won't stay long. We don't want to bother you," she said.

"I'm ready for a break. You've timed it just right." Abel tousled Paul's hair as he walked past the boy to his workbench. Emily watched as Abel quietly gathered up a set of sharp-looking chisels and set them carefully on a shelf out of the twins' reach. "Now, then. Look around all you like."

"But don't touch anything," Emily cautioned quickly.

"Don't worry about that. My carvings are meant to be handled. Phoebe and Paul can't hurt them."

"I hope you're right, but we'd better keep an eye on them just the same. Phoebe means well, but her enthusiasm gets the better of her a lot of the time. And if you turn your back on Paul, he'll be taking every machine in here apart to see how it works. Unfortunately he's not always successful at putting them back together." She was babbling.

"They'll be all right," Abel replied easily. "They're good, smart kids. They're welcome here anytime."

"Oooh, Mama," Phoebe called in an awed voice from the far corner of the workshop. "Look at this!"

Her daughter was standing in front of a life-size carving of a beautiful white-tailed buck. Emily felt Abel gently take the plate of apple bread out of her hands as she walked over to get a closer look.

The buck had been carved out of a single massive piece of wood, and he stood frozen on his pedestal in an alert pose as if he had just lifted his antlered head at an unexpected sound. Emily didn't know anything about wood carving, but even she could see how Abel had skillfully incorporated the gnarl of the wood into the shape of his final creation. It looked so lifelike that Emily reached out to touch it, forgetting her instructions to her children. She was almost surprised when she felt cool, hard wood beneath her fingertip instead of the warmth of a living animal.

From across the room, Abel watched Emily admire his buck for several minutes. He hesitated, then finally set down the plate and crossed over to stand beside her.

"He's incredible," Emily breathed. "I can't imagine the time this must have taken."

"He was a little troublesome," Abel agreed with a wry smile. "I traipsed around in the woods for months trying to catch glimpses of that particular whitetail so I could sketch him, and then the carving took close to nine months of steady work."

"I see it paid off." Emily indicated the huge blue ribbon tacked on to the side of the pedestal. "First place at the Georgia National Fair? That's impressive."

"Yeah, well." Abel felt embarrassed. "I'm generally not much for contests, but your grandma badgered me into it." He fingered the satin ribbon gently. "I guess you think it's kind of prideful keeping it tacked up like that, but nobody comes in here much but me. It's the first thing I ever won."

"You have every right to be proud of it, Abel. It's wonderful!"

He watched uncomfortably as she read the newspaper article he'd pinned up next to the ribbon. He'd kept that, too, because it was the first time a Whitlock had ever made the front page of the *Pine Valley Herald* for anything that wasn't a felony. God had done some mighty things in Abel's life, and this little corner reminded him of them. That was why he'd held on to the buck, even when people offered him crazy money for it. Whenever Abel looked at it, he felt a wave of gratitude and a fresh determination to use whatever talent he had to draw people's attention to the beauty God had sprinkled all around them. He had no words to explain that to Emily, though, and he worried that she'd think he was stuck on himself keeping all this out on display.

But that wasn't the only reason he'd just as soon she didn't look too hard at that article. The reporter had insisted on a photo of Abel standing next to the carving. Miss Sadie had hooted when she saw it. "The next time somebody points a camera at you, sonny, smile! You look like somebody just poked you with a stick."

"Look, Mama! It's our cow!" Abel felt a surge of relief as Phoebe called from across the room. "Come see!"

He followed as Emily walked over to the shelf her daughter was pointing to. When she saw what was on it, she glanced up at him and smiled. The animals of Goosefeather Farm marched along in miniature, one after the other. Beulah was there tossing her head, Glory had her neck and wings outstretched and Newman the tiny rooster had his feathers ruffled out. The rough shape of a goat was laid on its side next to the others, unfinished.

"I was making this set for your grandmother's birthday." He picked up the incomplete carving, weighing it in his hand. "I haven't had the heart to work on it since…lately."

Emily shook her head slowly. "Oh, Abel. It's too bad. Grandma would have loved them."

"Can I play with the little animals?" Phoebe asked hopefully.

"They aren't toys," Emily began, but Abel interrupted her smoothly.

"Of course you can, sweetheart. Here." He gathered the carvings up and handed them to Phoebe. She plopped happily down on the floor and began to chatter to herself as she moved the animals around.

"If Pheebs can play with that, can I play with this chess set?" Paul looked longingly at the intricately carved board and pieces that were set enticingly at his eye level.

"Paul just started learning how to play," Emily explained with a nervous smile.

"Sure. Help yourself. Your mom and I are going to have a cup of coffee, and I want to try some of this bread that smells so good."

"We won't be long," Emily repeated as he led the way over to a little table with a coffeemaker. The carafe was already half-full of inky liquid, and he took two of his mismatched mugs from the nearby cupboard and poured them each a cup.

"Stay as long as you like. You're not bothering me," he said, motioning for her to sit down on the bench that was pushed up against the log wall. He peeled up the foil that covered the plate and took a piece of the apple bread.

It tasted every bit as wonderful as it smelled. He closed his eyes and shook his head in appreciation as he chewed. "This is good. Really, really good."

"Thanks." The compliment seemed to settle her

nerves. "I'm glad you like it. Like Paul said, making up recipes is kind of a hobby of mine."

"If this is what you call a hobby, I think you should go pro." He took another big bite.

"I could say the same thing about you. I mean, I've seen you whittling, but I had no idea—" she gestured widely "—about all this. Your carvings are beautiful."

"I'm glad you like them."

"Do you ever sell your work?"

"Now and again," he replied evasively.

"Maybe you'd sell me one of your small pieces. I'd like to take something back to Atlanta with me."

Now, why was she spoiling a perfectly pleasant morning bringing that thought up? "I'll not take your money. If you see anything you'd like to have, take it as my gift, or I could make you something special if you want." Instantly he knew just what that would be. A slender branch of dogwood caught in blossom.

"That'd be nice if you're sure you don't mind," she said shyly. "But just something small. You know you should definitely find a market for these pieces."

"Like I said, I sell a few things here and there." Abel took another big bite of bread and hoped Emily wouldn't ask any more questions.

The truth was, his business was booming. He had more orders on his computer than he could fill in a year's time, and no matter how much he raised his prices, more commissions kept pouring in. Abel wasn't sure exactly how to handle that or how he felt about carving for money instead of for the joy of it.

It almost seemed dishonest to him to take so much money for something he loved to do, something he honestly couldn't help doing. When he picked up the right piece of wood, he saw the finished piece curled inside it, and he just couldn't rest easy until he'd chipped it free. The fact that people were willing to pay hundreds, even thousands, of dollars for his work was a genuine puzzlement to him.

"Well, we're taking up too much of your time. I'm sure you're wondering why I came," Emily began in a businesslike tone.

Abel smiled at her. He'd designed this workshop to catch the best and brightest of the available light, and the sunlight was now highlighting her hair, making its strands sparkle warmly. It traced the curve of her cheek and accentuated her features like only natural light could do. Unfiltered sunlight could be a harsh critic, but it loved Emily.

"No, I'm not wondering. I'm just glad you're here." It was true, he realized. Opening his workshop door to find Emily and her children on his doorstep had been as sweet and unexpected as finding a bluebird nest in a tangle of brambles.

She offered him an uncertain smile. "That's nice of you to say, especially considering how I've been acting." She firmed up her lips and looked him straight in the eye. "I came up here because I owe you an apology, Abel."

He shook his head. "No, you don't."

"I do. I realized it when Phoebe let the goats out. You couldn't have been any nicer to her about all that even though it took you forever to round them all back up. And you've been nothing but nice to me since I got here, and I've been fighting you at every turn. It's just…" She took a deep breath and forged on. "It's a little hard for me to trust people."

Well, that was an understatement. "People can disappoint you." He watched her expression carefully. They were treading on delicate ground.

"That's kind of the story of my life. But you've never disappointed me, and it isn't fair for me to treat you as if you have. Or will. So, I'm sorry."

"Don't worry about it. I never took it personally." He smiled encouragingly at her, trying to ease the concern he saw lingering in her eyes. "Although feel free to apologize to me any time if it involves a visit and some more of this bread."

"Do you really like it?" She looked shy and hopeful, and he felt his heart constrict a notch or two.

"You ask crazy questions." He helped himself to another piece.

"I have a reason for asking. I'm hoping we can work out a deal."

"Does this deal involve you cooking for me? Because if it does, I like it already."

"It does." She took a deep breath. "You're right. I'm not going to be able to handle the farm by myself. I really did think I'd learned enough during the summers I spent with Grandma to skate by until September, but I'm already in over my head."

"The simple life's not so simple."

"Exactly. So, I really need your help." Abel started to speak, but she held up her hand. "Let me finish, okay?"

"Okay." It looked like she had a whole speech planned out. He'd let her have her say. He took another bite of the sweet bread and settled in for the duration.

"The problem is I'm short on cash, and Grandma's funds won't be available to me until the end of the summer. No," she said when Abel tried to interrupt again.

"Let me get this out. I know you'll say you're willing to work for free. That's nice of you, but I can't accept it."

"Well, I've got my own reasons for wanting to help you out, Emily. You know what kind of reputation my family has around Pine Valley. Folks are going to think I conned your grandma into this deal."

Emily's mind flashed back to Bailey Quinn's comment, and she tilted up her chin. "Nobody who really knew my grandmother will believe that for a minute." She smiled. "Besides, you wouldn't let somebody work for you for free, would you?"

She had him there. "All right. We've laid out our problem well enough. Do you think you've found us a way around it?"

"Well, I was praying about it this morning, and I had an idea. Grandma has a pantry and a cellar both stuffed full of food. You know how she was. If it sat still long enough, she either canned it, froze it or dehydrated it. Putting up her harvest was the only thing she actually liked doing in the kitchen."

He laughed. "True."

Emily nodded. "And you told me the other day that you liked anything that you didn't have to cook yourself."

"Also true." He liked where this was going.

"So I thought maybe we could swap meals for chores. I could fix you a good, home-cooked supper every evening in exchange for your help. And I could send you home with plenty of baked goods for breakfast, too. If you're willing, that is."

He was perfectly happy to do her chores for nothing, and it was more than just his worry over what people were saying. He liked working at Goosefeather. He always had. He understood her wanting to trade it out, though, because he'd have felt the same way in her place. She was finally talking some sense.

Her idea was fine with him. He kind of liked the prospect of sitting across a table from Emily and the twins every evening, and the fact that she was so handy in the kitchen sweetened the deal even more. "I should warn you. I eat a lot."

She laughed. "I cook a lot, so we should be okay there. Do we have a deal?"

"Deal." He brushed crumbs off his fingers and held out his hand. She took it and gave it a brief shake, her dainty hand lost in his big one. He grinned at her. "Well, since you've already fed me breakfast today, it looks like I'm on the clock. What do you need me to do?"

"Mama needs you to go to the feed store with us so you can tell us what to buy." Paul walked over, his little face serious. "We're only used to buying people food." The little boy had carefully replaced the chessmen on the board, and Abel could see that every piece had been put back just where it went.

"All right. We'll go right now. We can take my truck. It'll make loading and unloading a lot easier." He didn't think there was any way they could load the feed they needed in the trunk of that tiny car Emily was driving, and the way the thing sputtered and groaned, Abel was afraid to tax it with any added weight. He made a mental note to take a look at the engine and see if he could tune it up a little. Emily was a mother with young kids, and she needed a reliable vehicle. The idea of a pretty woman like Emily stuck on the side of the road, especially up around Atlanta, made his skin crawl.

"Oh, no." Emily looked uneasy. "I don't expect you

to go now. You're working. We don't want to interrupt you. I mean, more than we already have."

"Mr. Abel likes being interrupted. He said so." Phoebe was holding a small carving of a fat little hen up to the light. "Can I have this one? I like it."

"Phoebe!" Emily sounded horrified, but Abel laughed.

"You can. If you promise to help your mama around the farm without fussing, I'll make you a whole flock of chickens if you want them."

"I'll try." Phoebe looked doubtful, but she crammed the little hen in her shorts pocket and nodded. "But I don't want just chickies. I want lotsa animals."

"Fair enough. And, Paul, if you'll do the same, that chess set can be yours at the end of the summer."

"Abel, that's too much! You don't have to…" Emily trailed off, looking at the joy shining on her son's face. The worry lines on her forehead softened a little. "Well. All right. Thank you, Abel. That's very generous of you. Paul has wanted a chess set of his own for some time now."

In Abel's opinion, any five-year-old boy who hankered after chess sets should have one. "Well, that works out fine, then. Do we have a deal, Paul?"

"Yes, sir! That's the best set I've seen anywhere," Paul said happily. "I'll take good care of it. I promise!"

"Okay, then. Let's get on to the feed store so your mama will have plenty of time to think up something good for supper."

For once in his life he'd said the right thing. The concerned lines smoothed out completely from Emily's brow, and she nodded. "Great. Let's go."

Chapter Six

"But, Mama, they're lonely! All their friends are gone. Can't we have them, please?"

Abel watched with amusement as Emily glanced from the two leftover chicks pecking around the cardboard box to the faces of her wheedling children. The twins had spotted the birds the minute they'd entered Lifsey's Feed and Seed, and Phoebe and Paul were bound and determined that the tiny things were coming to live on Goosefeather Farm.

"Won't be any more chicks now till next spring," Jack Lifsey said encouragingly. "These here are the last of the lot."

"*Pleease,*" Phoebe begged. "We can't just *leave* them here, Mama!"

"I don't see why we can't," Emily muttered. "Everybody else has."

"Tell you what," Lifsey said. "I'll let them go half price, seeing as how the kids like them so much. What about that?"

Emily sighed and looked over at Abel. "I don't know. What do you think?"

Abel blinked. The kids sensed the wind changing in their favor and immediately turned their begging eyes on him.

"Please, Mr. Abel? They can grow up and lay eggs for us and everything. Please?" Phoebe reached over and grabbed his hand, her little fingers twining over his. She blinked up at him imploringly with two big eyes that were exactly the shade as her mother's. Abel suddenly had a burning desire to buy the little girl every chicken in the state of Georgia. How did fathers do this?

"I don't think a cardboard box is a very healthy place for baby chickens to live," Paul said quietly. "Do you, Mr. Abel?"

Smart kid. There was no way to answer that question honestly that didn't involve riding home with two chickens in the back of his truck. Abel coughed, stalling for time. He glanced back over to Emily, trying to figure out what direction she wanted him to spin this. Emily shrugged.

"I don't know a thing about chickens. You're the farm guy. Your call."

His call. First she'd come all the way out to his cabin to apologize, then she offered him a seat at her supper table and now she was asking him to make a decision for her. This was way bigger than the two tiny chicks scuffling around in that cardboard box, and he knew it. She was trusting him, handing over tiny pieces of her life to him, and for Emily Elliott, that was one very big deal.

He knelt down next to the box and gave the chickens a closer look. They looked healthy and bright-eyed enough, so he turned his attention to the children. "They're mighty cute."

Two very eager nods.

"They aren't going to stay cute," he warned them. "All that downy fuzz is going to come off, and they're going to grow feathers. They're going to get kind of ugly there for a while."

"We don't care." Phoebe reached into the box and gently lifted up a peeping chick. "I'll still love you when you're ugly, I promise," she told the bird solemnly.

"And they're going to need a lot of looking after while they're little. You can't just chuck them in with the big chickens, because chickens aren't very smart and they'll peck these babies to death. We won't be able to put them in with the others until they're near about grown, and then we'll have to do it slow and careful."

Emily shuddered and rolled her eyes. "I knew there was a good reason I never liked chickens."

"We'll take care of them," Paul promised. "We'll feed and water them every day. You can show us how."

"You'll have to clean up after them, too." As if to prove his point, one of the chicks obligingly produced a mess on the newspaper lining the box. "Their brooder box will have to be cleared out every single day."

"We'll do that, too. We promise." Phoebe smiled winningly up at him, and Abel felt his willpower turn to jelly.

He figured the kids would get tired of the chicks pretty fast, but he also figured that taking care of helpless animals was a great way to learn about responsibility. He stood back up and nodded at Jack Lifsey. "We'll take them."

Two pairs of small arms were promptly flung around his legs, and he was hugged fiercely as the twins celebrated their win. Even grouchy Jack Lifsey was smiling as he watched the kids' excitement. "Ya'll can take that box with you to get them back to the farm, and you'd better add a bag of chick starter to your order, Abel."

"I'll load it, Jack. You figure up what we owe you, and I'll sign the slip."

"I'll sign for it," Emily said quickly. "This is all my responsibility now."

He'd always signed the slips for Miss Sadie, but Abel just shrugged and went over to hoist the fifty-pound sack of chick starter onto his shoulder. Emily was letting him help, and that was all that mattered right now. Let her fuss over signing the slip if it made her feel better.

He loaded the feed and got the kids settled in the back of the truck, the peeping chicks in their box between them. He opened the door for Emily and then glanced up to find Lifsey trying to catch his eye.

"Hey, Abel, can I talk to you a minute? Got something I need to ask you about." Lifsey looked uncomfortable, and Abel frowned.

"Sure. Here." He tossed Emily his keys. "Crank it up, and turn on the air. I won't be but a minute."

Lifsey led the way into the small office of the feed store and closed the door carefully behind them.

Abel's frown deepened. "What's wrong, Jack?"

"I didn't like to say anything in front of the lady. I didn't want to embarrass her in front of her kids and all. But, Abel, I can't let her sign Miss Sadie's slips."

"Why not? Miss Sadie always ran an account here."

"I know that, and she was one of my best customers. But Miss Sadie's gone now."

Abel wasn't getting it. "So what? You want Emily to open an account in her own name? That's not a problem. I'll bring her back in now, and we'll go ahead and get it done while we're here."

"Well, now, see?" Lifsey shifted his weight uncomfortably and avoided meeting Abel's eyes. "It *is* kind of a problem." The older man hesitated. "I can see you like the girl, and of course I know how much you thought of Miss Sadie. We all thought the world of her."

Abel narrowed his eyes. He didn't like the way this was going, not one bit. "Get to the point, Jack."

"Well, the truth is, the word around town is that Miss Emily isn't…particularly honest."

After a flash of disbelief, Abel felt something uglier, something he hadn't felt in a long while, start its slow burn in his belly. "I guess you'd better make yourself pretty clear about what you're trying to say here, Jack. And I'd choose my words mighty carefully if I were you."

Lifsey held his hands up. "Hold your horses, now! I'm not trying to rile you up, Abel. Like I said, I can see you've got a real soft spot for that girl, and I can't say as I blame you. She's pretty as a picture, and she seems just as sweet as sugar candy. But where there's a good bit of smoke, there's usually some fire. You know that as well as I do. I've heard the same thing from four or five folks. They're saying she was arrested back up in Atlanta for thieving."

Whatever nonsense he'd been expecting, it wasn't this. For a second Abel didn't know whether he wanted to punch Jack Lifsey in the nose or laugh out loud. He took a firmer grip on his faith and opted for the laugh. "I'd have thought you knew better than to listen to foolishness like that, Jack."

"Maybe it's foolishness, and maybe it isn't. Times

are tough, Abel, and business is business. I can't afford to extend credit to somebody I don't even know, especially when word from people I do know is that she's not trustworthy. I'm sorry, but I just can't do it."

Abel could hear the steady rumble of his truck outside, and he knew Emily would be wondering what was keeping him. If he tarried much longer, she was likely to pop back in to see what was going on.

He didn't want that to happen. She couldn't know about this. He wouldn't let a piece of silly small-town gossip hurt Emily, not when she was just starting to let down her guard a little bit. He'd been on the receiving end of talk like this often enough to know how it could set a person back. He stood silent for a minute thinking hard.

"Start me an account, then, Jack. You can do that, can't you?"

Relief spread across the store owner's face. "Well, sure, Abel! That's not a problem at all! And there's no limit on your credit here, neither." As Lifsey began tapping information into his computer, Abel shook his head slowly. Things sure had come to a strange pass in Pine Valley when a Whitlock could get all the credit he wanted, but Sadie Elliott's granddaughter was looked at sideways.

Lifsey clicked a couple more keys and looked up from the screen. "There we go. The account's all set up. And like I said, no limit. I know you're good for it."

Abel didn't answer Lifsey's smile. "If you had any sense, you'd know Emily's good for it, too, but we'll play it this way for now. At least you were smart enough not to say anything in front of her. We'll keep this between us. Understood?"

"Sure, if that's what you want." Lifsey nodded.

"And when you see whoever's talking about Emily, you make sure they know they're spreading lies. Emily Elliott never stole a thing in her life. You tell them I said so."

Emily opened her grandmother's cavernous oven and checked on her pot roast. It looked perfect, and the potatoes she'd added an hour ago were nicely browned. She poked one of them with a fork, nodded and grabbed two pot holders. Abel should be here any minute.

She levered the large chunk of meat onto a platter and clustered the seasoned potatoes, carrots and onions around it. She set it on the table, slid an apple crisp into the heated oven and then set about making gravy from the rich juices left in her roasting pan. She hummed as she worked. There was a lot to making a meal for a hungry man, but she'd take this any day over trying to milk a balky cow or being a midwife for a goat.

"Mr. Abel's here!" Phoebe's excited squeal made Emily jump, and she splashed hot gravy onto her wrist.

"Ouch! Good, that means it's suppertime. Wash up!"

She glanced up from the steaming gravy she was whisking as Abel came through the back door. He was wearing new dark jeans and a green cotton shirt that still looked like it had some of its factory creases. The damp ends of his dark hair were curling along its collar. He'd spruced up for this dinner, she realized. Her heart reacted oddly to the idea, bouncing around like a Ping-Pong ball.

"It sure smells good in here," he said with a crooked smile. He'd halted in the doorway, looking uncertain.

She smiled encouragingly back at him. "I figured

you for a meat-and-potatoes kind of guy, so I hope you weren't expecting a gourmet meal."

"Don't worry. This'll be plenty fancy to me."

"Take a seat, and I'll have it on the table in a jiffy." She quickly filled up her grandmother's gravy boat then she reached over and opened the smaller side oven to retrieve the pan of fluffy buttermilk biscuits.

Instead of sitting down, Abel crossed to the sink and washed his hands quickly. He came up beside her as she was picking the hot biscuits up with light, cautious fingers.

"I'll do that," he said, taking the napkin-lined basket out of her hands. "You're burning yourself." He picked up three of the biscuits at once and chucked them into the basket.

He was doing it again. "*Sit down*, I said." She pulled the basket out of his hands and thunked it down on the countertop. "You may be the boss of the barn, but I'm the boss of this kitchen. Sit."

Abel looked surprised and a little abashed, but he did what she said and took his place at the table.

Thankfully the children arrived in the kitchen just then. They talked over each other, eager to tell Abel rambling stories about their beloved chicks. He listened attentively as Emily finished piling golden biscuits in the basket. She set it in front of his plate along with a jar of her grandmother's homemade peach jam.

She stood back and surveyed her table nervously. It looked all right, didn't it? The red-checkered cloth was spotlessly clean and crowded with steaming dishes. Four places were neatly set with her grandmother's plain white plates, and she'd poured sweet tea over ice for the adults and glasses of fresh milk for the children. "I think we're ready to eat," she said. "Let's say grace. I think it's your turn tonight, Phoebe, isn't it?"

Her children settled in their seats and reached out their hands. She saw Abel startle slightly and then gently enclose the twins' small hands in his own and bow his head.

"Thank You, God, for this food Mama made except for the green beans because I don't like green beans." Emily's lips twitched as she listened to her daughter's sweet, high voice. "Thank You that Mr. Abel's here because we like Mr. Abel, and he got Mama to let us have our chickies. And bless our chickies to grow up and lay lots of eggs and not be roosters because roosters are mean. Amen."

"Amen," Abel agreed with a laugh he disguised as a cough. She glanced across the table and caught his blue eyes twinkling at hers. Her heart ping-ponged again, and she quickly dropped her gaze back down to her plate. *None of that*, she told herself firmly.

When Abel started on his second helping of roast, Emily relaxed in her seat with a sigh of relief. Her first meal was a hit. She listened to the happy chatter of her children and sipped her tea, wondering idly what would be the best choice for tomorrow's meal. Roast chicken, maybe? She made a good roast chicken. Although there was that casserole recipe she'd cut out of a magazine she was dying to try.

"Why don't you have any kids, Mr. Abel?" Paul's innocent question brought Emily back to high alert.

"Paul! Don't pester."

"He's not pestering." Abel wiped his mouth carefully with his napkin. "After spending some time with you two, I've been kind of wondering the same thing myself." He smiled, and her children grinned back, not noticing how neatly he'd sidestepped their question.

Emily noticed, though, and she turned the question over in her mind as her children and Abel finished eating. Why hadn't Abel ever married? She considered the man seated across from her. He was listening seriously as her daughter told him a wildly exaggerated tale about her chick and a caterpillar. Paul was growing impatient for his turn, and he tugged hard on Abel's sleeve. Without turning his head from Phoebe, Abel covered Paul's hand gently with his own and patted it, silently reassuring the boy that he would be next. Paul settled back down in his seat to wait, and Emily shook her head slowly.

The man was great with kids. Some woman should have snapped him up years ago and filled that cabin of his with a tribe of sturdy little black-haired children.

It could be he wasn't the marrying kind. Some men weren't, and Abel had always seemed to like his solitude more than most.

She was still pondering it later as she was washing the dishes. Abel had insisted on helping, and he was patiently drying each plate as she handed it to him, stacking them on the countertop in neat piles. He was being kind, but she really wished he'd sit down a nice safe distance away. Standing here right next to him made her feel…well, *crowded*, and the way their fingers kept brushing as she handed off each dish wasn't helping.

"So, why don't you?" she blurted out. "Have any children, I mean."

"Not married." Abel shot her a sideways glance, and his mouth quirked up. "Miss Sadie would have skinned me alive if…" He trailed off, his face coloring. "Aw. Emily, I'm sorry. I didn't mean anything by that."

He was so obviously upset that Emily had to laugh. She skimmed a handful of the foamy bubbles off the top of her dishwater and flung them at him. "Oh, quit choking. It's all right. Truth is, she came awfully close to skinning me alive the day I told her I was expecting. Not that I blame her."

Abel smiled faintly as he wiped the bubbles off his face, but his lean cheeks stayed brick red. "I'm sorry just the same, Emily. That's me. Any time I open my mouth I stick my boot straight in it. I do better when I don't talk. You want to know why I never got married? That's most of it right there. I just never got the hang of sweet-talking girls. I either bore 'em to death or make 'em mad every time." Emily made a scoffing noise, but Abel shook his head. "It's true. Last girl I took out for supper wanted me to take her home before we even got to the restaurant."

"You're kidding me!"

"Nope."

"Abel Whitlock! What on earth did you say to her?"

"Nothing much."

"You must have said *something*."

"Well…" He hesitated, looking guilty. "I told her she had ringworm. Well, now, she *did*," he said defensively when Emily began to sputter. "On her wrist. She probably caught it from her cat."

As Emily struggled not to laugh, she heard Abel protesting.

"I didn't think she'd get so upset over it. I even gave her some athlete's foot cream I had in the glove box of my truck."

Emily gave up and whooped helplessly, pressing her hands hard against her aching stomach.

"What?" Abel sounded genuinely bewildered. "Why's that funny? That clears it right up! Like I told her, I put it on the goats all the time."

Emily sank down to the floor, snorting. Above her Abel sighed heavily and added another dry plate carefully to his stack.

"Yeah," he said, shaking his head. "I do better when I don't talk."

Chapter Seven

"*Please, Mama?*"

Two weeks later Emily was once again looking from two pleading twins to Abel's face, this time in the front yard of the farmhouse. Abel was grinning that irresistible lopsided grin at her again, and some very inconvenient butterflies in her stomach were fluttering furiously. She fought to keep her frown in place, but the corners of her mouth kept tilting upward.

"We're not babies anymore, Mama." Paul sounded insulted.

"You'll always be *my* babies," Emily retorted automatically.

"But we don't want to go to town with you. The grocery store is boring. We want to stay here with Mr. Abel and play with our chickies." Phoebe set her chick down on the grass and watched as the small bird pecked curiously at a green blade.

As usual Abel had known what he was talking about. The cute little downy balls of fluff had turned into gangly, half-feathered birds almost overnight, but the twins' affection for them hadn't wavered. Chickadee and Puff were still perfect as far as the twins were concerned. It warmed Emily's heart to see how tenderly her children cared for the ugly little birds, but she also worried that it was going to be awfully hard for the twins to leave them behind at the end of the summer.

"I'll be glad to keep an eye on them, Emily, and it'd probably be easier for you to run your errands without them. Wouldn't it?" Abel lifted an eyebrow at her, and she almost laughed out loud. Easier to run errands without two bored five-year-olds in tow? Understatement of the century.

She was tempted, but she knew better than most that when one person shrugged off responsibility, somebody else had to take it up. Her children were most definitely her responsibility, not Abel's. "They'll slow *you* down, though. And I'm sure you've got plenty planned out to do this morning. Too much probably. I'm afraid you're working too hard."

"Have to earn my keep." He smiled again, and his blue eyes, just the color of the shirt was wearing, sparkled. "I feel like I should be pulling longer hours to pay for the food I'm getting. I haven't eaten this good in…well, ever."

That did it. Emily lost her battle with the corners of her lips, and she could feel a foolish smile spreading across her face. Ever since that first pot roast, Abel had been unfailingly enthusiastic about her cooking, and she had to admit it was nice to feed an appreciative man. Last night she'd even tried the new casserole recipe on him, and he'd raved over it. More important, he'd eaten three generous helpings.

Talk was cheap, but three helpings meant something.

"Anyhow, these two don't slow me down all that

much," Abel continued. His expression warmed as he glanced down at her children. "Truth is, I've gotten used to having them around. I get kind of lonesome when they're not here."

"See? Mr. Abel gets lonely without us." Phoebe smirked up at her mother.

"Yeah," Paul inserted, picking up his chicken and putting her down gently in a more desirable patch of grass. "It's sad to be lonely. We should stay here."

Abel reached over and rumpled the boy's blond hair with an affectionate hand. Paul grinned up at the tall man, and Emily's heart gave a leap and lodged itself solidly in her throat. Lately those little interactions between man and boy were becoming more and more common, and Emily couldn't decide whether to be thankful or concerned.

It warmed her heart to see her children, particularly her son, behaving so naturally with Abel. Paul was starved for adult male companionship, and he was drinking up Abel's attention like a thirsty little sponge. And Phoebe had only to blink her big eyes in Abel's direction, and Emily could see every bit of the big man's willpower melt like a pile of sugar in the rain. The little girl adored Abel and followed him around the farm like a puppy.

That was all fine for now, but she could see trouble coming. Abel was a good man and a kind one, but this relationship the twins were coming to rely on had a built-in expiration date. She was afraid the chicks weren't going to be the only thing the twins would find hard to leave behind in Pine Valley.

But today the sun was shining, and her morning chores were all done. Her children were happy and healthy, and the end of the summer was still a good while away. Abel was looking at her with a hopeful gleam in his eyes, so she gave in.

"All right. If you're sure and if the twins promise to behave themselves."

There was an immediate flurry of happy promises, and Phoebe squeezed her chick so enthusiastically that it peeped in protest and had to be rescued.

Phoebe's face crumpled. "I didn't mean to hurt her!" she cried as Abel inspected the chick carefully.

"You didn't. She's okay. She just didn't like being squeezed. Tell you what, I'll carve you a little chick just like Puff here to go with your hen, and you can squeeze her to your heart's content."

"Cool! When?" Paul immediately went on high alert, a calculating gleam in his little eye. He was fascinated with Abel's carving, and he'd been fingering Phoebe's wooden hen ever since they left the workshop.

"How about now? I've got some tools in my truck and a little hunk of wood that I was just thinking looked an awful lot like a baby chick."

"Can I watch?" Phoebe wanted to know.

"Can I help?" Paul asked at the same time.

Abel laughed. "Yes and yes. If that's all right with your mom, I mean." He glanced up at Emily.

She hesitated, torn between a mental image of cuts needing stitches and the hope shining on Paul's face. "I guess so. But be careful and do just what Mr. Abel tells you!"

"Thanks, Mama!" He clenched his arms tightly around her in an enthusiastic hug.

Abel walked with her to her little car. Emily was so distracted by the man striding beside her that she forgot to watch where she was going and stumbled clumsily over a clump of tough grass.

"Careful there," he murmured, reaching out a strong hand to catch her elbow. He leaned over and pulled the car door open. "I took a look at this engine for you yesterday evening while you were cooking supper," he said. "I added some oil, but it needs a good tune-up. I'll get to it this afternoon when you get back."

Emily frowned as she slid into the hot seat. "Fixing my car wasn't part of our agreement. Of course, for that matter, neither was babysitting." Maybe this wasn't such a good idea after all.

"I've got to do a little something extra to pay you back for that lemon pie you made last night. If that wasn't going above and beyond, I don't know what is." One side of his mouth tilted up. "Anyhow, I like tinkering. And spending time with the twins."

A burst of childish laughter came from the yard. One of the little chicks must have done something funny. Emily loved to hear her children laughing. When she saw the echo of her own affectionate smile on Abel's face, her heart bobbed and dipped crazily, and she felt her cheeks start to burn.

She'd never had anybody in her life before to share parenting moments with, and there was something about the intimacy of it that unsettled her, making her feel like all her most vulnerable spots were unprotected.

She had to get out of here. "Whew. It's hot," she said brightly, and reached over to start the ignition.

Abel's smile faded, and he leaned closer so she could hear him over the noisiness of the engine. "Listen, Emily, don't worry. I'll keep both eyes on the twins while you're gone. They're safe with me."

She knew it was true. He would keep her babies safe because he was that kind of a man. He was so close she caught the aroma of wood shavings that always seemed to cling to him, and she could smell the faint scent of the coffee she'd made earlier on his breath. Her eyes dipped down to his mouth—a mouth that somehow melded strength and gentleness in its crooked smile— and suddenly she found herself wondering what those lips would feel like on hers.

What was she doing? Emily snatched her gaze away guiltily and focused hard on the dashboard clock. "Wow! Look at the time! I'd better get going if I want to be back in time to fix lunch."

The clock hadn't worked since she bought the car, but hopefully he hadn't noticed that yet.

"Yeah. Yeah, I think you'd better get going." There was a strange tone in his voice, and when Emily dared another glance back up, she saw a stunned intensity in Abel's eyes that struck her like an electric shock.

Emily flashed him a mechanical smile, banged the car door closed and barreled down the gravel drive, her heart pounding like a jackhammer.

This was bad. Those silly little sparks that were flashing between them weren't as one-sided as she'd assumed. Abel was feeling them, too, and that could only mean one thing.

Trouble.

"Wow." Paul settled next to Abel on the top step of the farmhouse porch, carefully holding the square of sandpaper he'd been entrusted with. "How do you do that?"

Abel shaved off another sliver of wood with his carving knife. The little chick was taking shape. "Well, now, it's hard to explain. I've always been able to do it. I never could understand why everybody can't, but I guess it's like singing. I can't sing, but other folks sure can. It's just the way God made us, I reckon."

"Mama can sing." Phoebe picked up a curl of fragrant wood and twisted it around her stubby little finger.

"I know." A memory flitted back through Abel's mind like a hummingbird zipping past. As a teenager, Emily used to sing while she cooked. He remembered snatches of her songs drifting out of the half-open kitchen window. He'd listened while he'd weeded the garden. "I've heard her. She has a real pretty voice."

"Mama doesn't sing much anymore. I guess she likes cooking better now." Paul spoke without taking his eyes off Abel's hands. "Can you teach me to do that?"

"Teach you to carve?" Abel considered. "Well, for this kind of carving you've got to have some really sharp knives, so I guess we'd better check with your Mama first. But if she's willing, I am."

"Maybe she'll let me if you say it's all right." Paul sounded hopeful. "She worries a lot, but she likes you."

"Well..." Abel floundered for something to say. "That's good. I like all of you, too. Very much. Now, see this little piece sticking out here? I'm fixing to make it Puff's little beak."

His trick worked. Both twins leaned in closer to watch the tiny beak emerge from the wood. They dropped the subject, and Abel was glad.

He'd never been much for conversation, but to his surprise he'd found talking to the twins easy. Not today, though. Today he didn't particularly want to chat with Emily's children about how much he liked them. The truth was, he was starting to figure out that he cared about all of them a little too much.

Especially Emily.

It had been lurking around in the back of his mind for the last couple of weeks, this feeling that was a mixture of longing and hoping and something else he wasn't quite ready to put a name to. Last night he'd felt it again when he joined them for supper at Miss Sadie's big oval table. He'd seen his place set just as if he belonged there. There'd even been a sprig of fresh mint set beside his napkin because Emily knew he liked mint in his tea.

He'd been keeping a lid on those feelings as best he could, but it wasn't easy. He'd always had a soft spot for her. He knew that as well as anybody else. He'd even spent a fair amount of time years ago daydreaming about scenes just like last night's supper table.

Of course he'd had enough sense to know Emily was out of his reach. He knew the gap that separated families like the Whitlocks from decent ones like the Elliotts. He'd been reminded of it often enough by other folks in Pine Valley over the years. Miss Sadie might act like there was no difference between them, but Abel knew where the line was, even if she didn't.

Or he'd thought he did. He had to admit sitting down to supper with Emily night after night had blurred that line some. Then today out by the car, she'd smiled at him, and her eyes had dropped down to his mouth and she'd gone all nervous. A pretty little blush had crept up her neck to stain her cheeks, and that old longing had risen up in him until it had blocked out everything else.

He'd wanted to kiss her just then more than he'd ever wanted anything he could remember. And unless he was sorely mistaken, Emily had been thinking about kissing him, too. That alone was incredible enough that he'd felt the jolt of it clear down to his boots. In fact, he wasn't sure he'd recovered yet, and he'd been sitting on this porch step for the better part of two hours since then.

He heard the crunch of tires on gravel, and he looked over, expecting to see Emily's dinged-up little car creeping up the drive. Instead he saw Jacob Stone's pickup truck.

Abel got slowly to his feet, brushing a snowfall of wood shavings off his jeans, and handed the finished chick to Phoebe, who clutched it happily. Then he reached up and stowed his carving knife safely on a ledge of wood at the top of the porch column. That'd keep the little ones away from it while he talked with Stone.

Although he didn't imagine the pastor had driven all the way out to Goosefeather Farm to talk to him. He'd have gone to the cabin for that. Unless Abel missed his guess, it was Emily who Stone was looking for, and it must be something pretty important to lure the busy preacher this far out of town on a weekday morning.

Emily pulled up to the farmhouse and frowned. There was a strange truck parked in the driveway, and Abel and another man were standing on the front porch talking with the twins milling around their feet. Abel had one hand gently resting on Phoebe's shoulder. Emily wrestled her gaze away from that appealing picture and forced herself to focus on the visitor. Was that the minister?

Abel left the porch and met her at the car. "I'll get the groceries on into the kitchen. The preacher seems to want to have a talk with you."

"With me?"

"So he says. I'll keep an eye on the twins for you."

"Okay. Thanks." She walked toward the porch, where Pastor Stone was talking easily to her children. When he saw her approaching, the minister straightened up and smiled.

He had a nice smile. When you added in the dimples that carved deep brackets around his mouth and his slightly untamed-looking mop of curly blond hair, he presented quite a package. It was no wonder that Pine Valley Community Church was attracting record numbers of young single women these days.

Jacob Stone wasn't just eye candy, though. Emily had heard him preach a few times when she went to church with the twins, and the man had a gift. His sermons married spiritual and practical concepts so well that you never saw the seam between them. But none of that explained why he was waiting at her door. Or why he was looking more than a little uncomfortable.

"Emily, I sure hope I haven't come at a bad time."

"Not at all. Abel said you wanted to talk to me?" She left the sentence hanging on a question mark.

"I do." Jacob Stone nodded several times, ran one hand through his hair and glanced around uneasily. "In private, if that wouldn't be too much of an imposition."

Emily felt a twinge of nervousness. This couldn't be good. "Sure. Come on in. Grandma's got a parlor that's been entertaining ministers for decades now. In fact, you've probably spent more time in it than I have."

Stone laughed as he followed her through the screen door into the living room. They took a left into the small parlor with its stiff Victorian furniture and carefully placed knickknacks. Emily cringed when she saw the film of dust on the varnished tables. Another thing she hadn't found the time to do. That list was getting lengthy.

Stone closed the door not quite shut behind them. Emily felt a little surge of amusement mingled with pity. She imagined that a good-looking minister like Stone would have to be more careful than most. Shutting himself up with a single woman in any room would be an invitation for the church gossips.

Especially when the woman had an unmarried pregnancy in her past. The thought sneaked past Emily's defenses, but she tilted her chin up a notch and forced a smile as she motioned for the minister to have a seat in the pleated armchair across from her.

She'd made her peace with her past and with God. What other people thought about it was really none of her business.

Jacob Stone shifted on his chair and coughed. "I don't want to hold you up any longer than I have to, so I guess I'd better get to my point."

"All right." She nodded and braced herself, wondering what on earth was going on.

"I'm afraid your name's been tangled up in some gossip. I was hoping it would die down, but instead it seems to be gaining momentum. It's been worrying me a good bit. I've been praying about it, and I think it'd be best all the way around if you and I deal with it head-on."

"Gossip about me?" Emily blinked. "I haven't heard of it. And I honestly can't think what it could be about. All I've done since I got here is try to manage these crazy animals and keep the farm going, nothing that would start any tongues wagging. I've barely even been to town except to buy groceries and animal feed. Unless..." A thought occurred to her, and a chill settled over her heart. "Does this gossip concern my past?"

The minister met her gaze squarely and nodded once. "It does."

"I see." Emily tilted her chin up another notch. "Then the story you've been hearing is true. I got pregnant when I was nineteen. I was living here with my grandmother for the summer, and I had a romance with a local boy. We were both young and foolish, and we paid the price for that. Or I did. He and his family didn't choose to be involved."

"That must have been hard for you. But—" Pastor Stone began.

Emily interrupted. "That was before I found my own faith. Of course now I see things differently, and I make different choices. But you should know I'll never regret having my twins no matter how they came to me. I've made plenty of mistakes in my life, but I don't count my children among them." Her voice wobbled a little at the end, and two fat tears splashed down her cheeks. She dashed them away quickly. She would *not* cry about this.

"No." The pastor's eyes drifted toward the window. White Priscilla curtains were looped back on either side of the glass framing a view of the front yard. Paul and Phoebe were busy chasing each other around the yard playing some twin-invented version of tag. "They most certainly are not mistakes. In fact, I think they're beautiful examples of what God can do when we trust Him with our challenges."

Emily nodded. He was right. Trusting God hadn't come easily to her, but she was slowly learning that God always worked things out for good. Just as she started to relax a little in her seat, a male voice spoke tightly from the doorway.

"If you're done upsetting Emily, Stone, maybe you can think of something back at the church that needs your attention right about now."

"Abel!" As Emily stared, Abel pushed the door wide open and stood on its threshold, his blue eyes icy hard.

She'd only seen him this angry once before, and that had been years ago when he caught two of the town's rowdier teenagers chucking rocks at an injured dog on the side of the road. He'd had the same look on his face that afternoon that he did now, and Emily understood why the boys had turned tail and run when they saw Abel getting out of his pickup that day.

Abel took a step into the room, his expression dark. "I'm going to speak plain because I don't want any misunderstanding between us. I don't generally make a habit of listening at doors, preacher, and I don't think much of people who do. But I'm not sorry I heard what I did, not if it puts a quicker stop to it. You're upsetting Emily by raking up the past, and I'll not stand here for it, not for a minute. I'll not see her judged by you or any other man."

Stone detached his stunned gaze from Abel and turned to face her. "If I upset you, Emily, or made you feel judged, please accept my apologies. It surely wasn't my intention."

"Of course not! No apology necessary. Abel, you should mind your own business." Emily felt flustered and uneasy.

Abel spoke quietly, but there was something in his gaze when he looked at her that made her cheeks flush hotly red. "You can get mad if you want to, Emily, but like I said, I'm not about to stand by and let any man, preacher or not, come in here and worry you." Abel looked back at Stone, his lips thin. "Am I making myself clear?"

Stone met Abel's hot gaze calmly. It seemed the preacher had a little backbone of his own. "Why don't you come in and sit down, Abel? You obviously care about Emily, and believe it or not, so do I. In any case, you might as well stop glowering at me. I've come out here to get this out in the open so it can be dealt with, and I plan to do just that."

"You've said your piece, and I've said mine. I don't see what else there is to talk about." Abel kept his place by the door.

"Abel, *stop it*." Emily glared at him before turning her attention back to Jacob Stone. "I'm so sorry about this."

"Don't worry about it. You're a blessed woman to have such a loyal friend, even if he is awfully busy barking up the wrong tree at the moment. Now, if you'll both let me finish, here's the thing. You jumped the gun on me, Emily. The gossip that's going around town doesn't have anything to do with your pregnancy years ago. At least—" the minister paused, appearing to think a moment before continuing "—not directly. As it happens, it's about something very different."

Emily frowned, momentarily distracted from Abel's behavior. "I don't understand."

"You may not, but I think I do." Abel came in the parlor and shut the door behind himself a little harder than seemed absolutely necessary. "If you'd come to me, Stone, I could have told you it was all a bunch of nonsense. There was no need to bother Emily with it."

"Bother Emily with what?" Emily looked from one man to the other. "What's a bunch of nonsense? What's going on? What are people saying?"

The pastor flicked an uneasy look from Abel's face to Emily's before he answered, "An…individual…has been telling people in town that you have a criminal record for theft. They've been warning store owners not to extend any sort of credit to you."

Emily's heart sank down to the pit of her stomach and sat there like a lump of concrete. Certain subtle little things slipped tellingly into place. "I see."

"They've been pretty convincing, I'm afraid. As a matter of fact, I'm surprised you haven't noticed the backlash from it in town."

Emily remembered the wary looks she'd been given at the grocery store and the cashier's reluctance to accept her out-of-town debit card. "I have, actually. I just didn't recognize it for what it was."

"Anybody with a grain of sense would know this is nothing but a mess of lies, and I don't think much of your coming out here to badger Emily about this, Stone. You'd have been better off paying a call on the person who's spreading this nonsense. And I can tell you one thing for sure and certain. If you don't speak with them soon, I will."

"Abel." Emily spoke more sharply than she meant to. Her mind raced as she tried to decide what to say and how to approach this unexpected development. She wasn't coming up with any particularly attractive options at the moment. "I've told you before I can handle my own problems."

"I've already spoken to the individual in question. Well," the pastor amended, "actually the individual spoke to me because Emily has been attending church with us for the past few weeks. Something I very much hope you'll continue to do, by the way." He smiled at her. "This person and I had a very…uncomfortable conversation in my office yesterday. I'm afraid I didn't react quite as I was expected to. The…individual was quite upset with me."

"You're being mighty charitable about not putting a name to all this lying, Stone. I think Emily has a right to know who's spreading this garbage about her." Abel speared Stone with a sharp look. "Seems only right to me."

"I really don't think—" Stone began, but Emily interrupted, holding up one hand.

"That's all right. I already have a pretty good idea. And if it's who I think it is, you've certainly got your hands full. Please don't cause yourself trouble on my account, Pastor Stone." She swallowed hard. "Especially since there's some truth in what she's telling people."

"Well, she's stretching whatever truth she's telling." Abel frowned. "I've known you since you were fourteen. I think I know you well enough to know you're no thief, and I understand better than Stone how gossip works. There's been plenty of talk about me and my family over the years, and whatever truth there was to it always got spiced up a good bit in the telling."

She glanced up at him and winced. He looked so sure.

This was harder than she'd thought, but that didn't matter. She still had to do it. And maybe she could kill two birds with one stone and douse those sparks kindling between them now, too.

Chapter Eight

The room instantly fell silent. The only sounds Abel could hear were the ticking of a clock and the happy shouts of the twins out in the front yard.

"I don't believe it," he said finally. He didn't. He knew Emily Elliott, and he was convinced that she would never take anything that wasn't legally hers. She wasn't that kind of woman.

She couldn't be.

"You might as well believe it, because it's true." Emily's face was pale with those two bright red spots burning high on her cheeks like they always did when she was ruffled. "It's not something I'm proud of, but I'm not going to lie about it."

"You don't owe us an explanation, Emily," Pastor Stone said quietly. "You're not in the wrong here. Whatever mistakes you made in your past, God's forgiven you for them. Someone who calls herself a Christian has no business trying to hurt you with them."

Emily sighed. "Lois Gordon doesn't want me back in Pine Valley—even temporarily. I guess she's doing her best to make sure I don't stay any longer than I have to.

Sorry, but we all know who's behind this. Mrs. Gordon took a dislike to me when I dated her son, Trey, and it got worse after…after the twins."

Pastor Stone didn't bother to deny the accuracy of her guess. "Lois has been through a lot of tragedy these last few years. She never got over losing Trey in that accident. Unfortunately she's the kind of person who's the hardest for me to help, mainly because she doesn't believe she needs any." Jacob Stone sighed and ran a hand through his hair, standing it up on end. "She's in pain, and hurting people are always the ones who hurt others."

"Well, there's some truth in what she's telling people no matter what her motivation might be." Emily met Abel's eyes squarely. "Six years ago I was arrested in Atlanta for shoplifting. It wasn't the first time I'd done it, either. It was just the first time I got caught."

The twins' yelling outside had shifted from playful to angry, and Abel gratefully took the escape route it offered him. "I'll go see to the twins and let you two finish your talk," he said and left before either of them could argue.

Phoebe and Paul were squabbling over the rules to their tag game. Abel listened for a few minutes, then helped them strike a bargain that seemed to work well enough. They ran back off to play, and Abel lowered himself onto the step and watched them, grateful for a few minutes alone.

He felt a little stunned and more than a little ashamed at the way he'd taken on the preacher and Jack Lifsey about Emily. He'd been so sure that she was innocent. There hadn't been a shred of doubt in his mind.

It looked like he'd been wrong about her, and that

spooked him a little. He'd never thought he was a man who'd make a fool over himself about a woman because he couldn't see her clearly enough. He remembered trying to talk sense into his brother, Danny, when he fell hard for Missy Wyatt in twelfth grade. Abel knew Missy well enough to know that the girl was nothing but trouble in a real pretty package, but Danny sure hadn't been able to see it until he'd caught her in the school parking lot kissing his best friend. By that time, everybody had known what was going on except for Danny himself, and they'd tried to tell him. He just hadn't been willing to listen.

Abel remembered some of the sharp words he'd been throwing around and winced. He came from generations of hot-tempered men with big mouths and shady ideas of right and wrong, and he'd had to work hard to shake off the reputation they'd saddled him with. He wanted to be known in Pine Valley as a man who told the truth, whose handshake was as good as a legal paper and who could be relied upon to be reasonable and fair. Acting foolish over a woman wasn't going to help him with any of that.

The trouble was that all of this mattered way too much to him—what Emily had done in the past, what kind of woman she was now, how she thought and what she felt. They mattered because those were the kinds of things a man had to consider when...well, when he looked at a woman the way he'd started looking at Emily.

Abel didn't know which thing shook him up more: the fact that the rumors about Emily had turned out to be at least partly true or that somehow he'd gotten to the point that he was thinking about Emily Elliott the way a man thought about the woman he wanted to spend the rest of his days with.

The door opened behind him, and Emily and Stone came out on the porch. Abel got to his feet but kept his eyes focused on the twins, who were running circles around the oak tree in the front yard.

"I don't know." Emily's voice sounded strange, and Abel darted a quick look over at her face. She was still pale except for those bright red spots on her cheeks, but there was something new in her face now, a kind of worried sparkle. "I'm still not sure this is a good idea."

"I think it's a great idea." Stone sounded confident. "In fact, I think it's more than that. I believe in God, not coincidences. You've got experience working in a coffee shop, and the church just started a brand-new one that's floundering. It's perfect." The preacher flashed a grin at Emily. "To tell you the truth, I've got a personal reason for being excited about it. Grounds for Faith is my baby. I thought a church-sponsored coffee shop would be a great opportunity for outreach and fellowship, and I've got a lot of friends pastoring churches in other areas who've done similar things with great results. But a lot of the older members of the congregation have some serious reservations about the whole idea, and the fact that the shop hasn't really taken off hasn't helped. I think you're an answer to some pretty desperate prayers."

"It sounds awfully tempting."

"Well, spend some time thinking and praying about it and give me a call in a day or so to let me know what you decide. And don't fret yourself between now and Sunday. You're doing the right thing."

Emily worried her lower lip with her teeth. "Do you really think it'll do any good?"

"Who knows? One thing I've learned in this job is you never know what God will do if you put all your eggs in His basket. Now, I'd better be getting on back to the church before my secretary sends out a search party." He turned to Abel and held out his hand. "Whitlock."

Abel shook it firmly. "I'll walk you to your truck," he said. Stone raised an eyebrow but nodded.

When they were out of Emily's earshot, Abel spoke. "Looks like I owe you an apology."

"Not the way I figure it. You were just looking after Emily." The pastor shot him a thoughtful look. "You've got your reasons for that, I guess. You do seem to have kind of a hair trigger where judgment is concerned, though."

"I have my reasons for that, too, I reckon."

"So I gathered. Funny. Everybody I know around here speaks highly of you. You've got yourself a fine reputation in Pine Valley."

"You've not been here long. It wasn't always that way."

"Maybe not, but it is now. Could be I'm not the only one raking up the past around here. You could stand a dose of your own advice." Stone clapped him on the back. "See you both on Sunday."

Abel walked back to the porch, and he and Emily watched as Stone slowly navigated his truck down the bumpy gravel driveway. The twins headed for the barn, taking their chicks and their chatter with them. Abel felt like a coiled spring, as if he was about to jump straight out of his skin. He couldn't look at Emily, but he was aware of exactly where she stood beside him.

"Pastor Stone wants me to help them get the church coffee shop established," Emily told him, "but don't worry. If I decide to do it, it's only part-time. I'll be home in plenty of time to cook supper, so I can keep up our end of the deal. And the twins can go to the summer day care program the church is running for free since I'd be a church employee."

She obviously expected him to say something. "Sounds like something you'd be good at." He didn't like the idea, he realized. Not only would it mean Emily would be spending a good chunk of time away from the farm, but she'd be seeing a lot more of Jacob Stone into the bargain. He liked Stone well enough, but women flocked to him like bees to honeysuckle. Abel didn't much like the idea of the preacher and Emily working together.

Emily was gazing over the fields thoughtfully. "It almost sounds too good to be true. It kind of worries me."

Everything worried Emily. Abel let a few uncomfortable seconds of silence pass. "Green beans need picking," he said finally. "I'd best get on that."

"Could it wait a few minutes? I think maybe we need to talk." He felt her hand reach out and touch his arm, and he jumped. This woman had every nerve he owned on edge.

"Abel, would you look at me, please?"

He raised his eyes to meet hers. The hopeful look he'd seen on her face a few moments ago had faded. Now her gray-green eyes looked troubled and tired, and the hurt he saw lurking there flopped his heart right over.

"I owe you an explanation." She swallowed and tilted her chin upward, and something about that familiar, brave little gesture pushed him right back over the edge he was teetering on.

This was Emily. Nothing else mattered much. "You don't have to explain anything to me."

"I think maybe I do. Pastor Stone said you've been standing up for me all over town." She swallowed, and he saw a suspicious shimmer in her eyes. "You're probably regretting that right about now."

"Nope." He realized the truth of it as he spoke. He reached out and took both her small hands in his. "I'd do it again. I *will* do it again if I hear any more of this foolishness."

"What they're saying about me is true. Lois may have her own reasons for broadcasting it all over, but I'm responsible for what I did. And I did do it, Abel."

He nodded. "I heard you. And I won't deny that it threw me for a minute, but I'll tell you why it did. Whoever you were back then, you're not that person anymore. The Emily I know would no more take something that didn't belong to her than I would. God's seen to that. So whatever happened in the past doesn't matter." He was speaking to himself as much as he was speaking to her. Maybe the preacher had a point.

"It means a lot to me that you think that way." Emily swallowed hard. As he watched, a single tear streaked down her face, and she reached up to scrub it away impatiently with the back of her hand.

The tear did it, that and the tiny quiver of her lips. It was that combination that pushed him past whatever reserve he had left where Emily Elliott was concerned.

He stopped thinking, leaned over and covered her soft mouth gently with his own.

He kept the kiss simple, then drew back slowly, gauging her reaction. She looked stunned. Whatever she'd been expecting him to do, it hadn't been that.

He couldn't say the thought of kissing her had never crossed his mind before, but he was pretty sure it was a new idea for her.

As far as he was concerned, though, it was perfect. As he looked down into her face, he felt a flood of possessiveness wash over him. He'd never wanted anything as much as he wanted this, all of it, this woman, her twins, this brambly old farm. This was every hope he'd ever had wrapped up in one sweet package.

"Abel." Emily's voice came out a little uneven, and his lips quirked up. He'd flustered her. He kind of liked that.

"Mmm?"

"I think…" Emily started, then stopped.

He raised his eyebrows at her and waited. She swallowed, moistened her lips and tried again.

"I think you should go pick those green beans now." She nodded firmly and retreated into the house, letting the screen door flap shut behind her with a loud bang.

On Sunday Emily sat nervously in her pew as Pastor Stone welcomed visitors and went through a lengthy list of announcements. Only he and Emily knew that the special testimony listed in the church bulletin would be hers.

Even Abel didn't know. He was sitting next to Phoebe, and she was grateful for her daughter's squirmy little body between them. Ever since that kiss on the front porch, she'd been keeping her distance. So far she'd been successful. Abel hadn't made any effort to close the gap, but there was something in his face that told her that sooner or later he would.

She wasn't entirely sure how she felt about that. Not that the kiss hadn't thrilled her all the way to her toes. It definitely had. The problem was she wasn't sure how she felt about that, either.

The woman in front of her coughed, bringing Emily abruptly back to the present. She couldn't believe she was sitting here in church thinking about kissing Abel. She felt a blush stain her cheeks, and she darted an uneasy look in his direction. He caught her eye, and the corner of his mouth twitched as if he knew exactly what she was thinking. As if maybe he was thinking something along the same lines himself.

That didn't help. Emily quickly looked back down at the paper bulletin in her hands. It was trembling slightly, and she didn't know if that was because she was going to get up and speak in front of this whole congregation in about two minutes or because she couldn't decide if she wanted the man sitting between her twins to kiss her again or not.

This was all so complicated. Emily felt a rush of longing for her tough, straightforward Atlanta life. Since she'd come to Goosefeather Farm, everything felt twisted and hard to figure out. It wasn't just the farming thing, either, although she sure wasn't getting much better in that department. It was even more than her confusion about Abel.

Here in Pine Valley, the past she desperately wanted to put behind her kept looping around and jostling the present. Now the future had started whispering promises that she couldn't bring herself to believe. Happily-ever-afters just weren't that easy to come by. She'd learned that the hard way. She rubbed at her eyes and sighed. This whole situation made her tired.

Pastor Stone's tone changed, and Emily refocused her attention on the service. He'd finished the announcements and was addressing his congregation.

"You all know that now and again we make time for special testimonies, and you'll see in the bulletin that we have one of those scheduled this morning. I've invited Miss Emily Elliott to speak to us. Emily is the granddaughter of our beloved Mrs. Sadie Elliott, and if you don't know her already, you soon will because she's agreed to help us get our new coffee shop off the ground. Since she's going to be working for the church part-time, I thought it would be beneficial for all of us to hear her story. Emily?"

Jacob Stone offered her an encouraging smile, and Emily stood up, feeling her knees shaking like jelly as she began to sidle her way down the pew to the aisle. As she passed Abel, he reached out with one hand and caught her arm.

Startled, she glanced down at him. His face was set and drawn, and his eyes bored into hers. Abel spoke quietly and intensely. "I don't know what Stone's talked you into, Emily, but listen to me. *You do not have to do this.*"

She felt heat flare into her pale cheeks, and she lifted her chin. "Yes, Abel, I think I do." On legs that suddenly seemed sturdier, she made her way up to the pulpit.

As Emily looked out into the church, some of her nervousness returned. The pews were packed. Well, maybe it was better this way. She'd tell everybody at once and get it over with.

"A lot of you have been hearing stories about me having some dishonesty in my past, maybe even criminal behavior. I'm here to tell you that the things you've been hearing, in part at least, are true."

Her eyes skimmed over the congregation, picking out faces. There were her children looking innocently interested. They knew her stories, and there would be no surprises for them today, thank goodness. Abel was not looking at her but was looking down at the hands he had clenched in his lap. She saw Jack Lifsey from the feed store, but he wouldn't meet her eyes, either. Bailey Quinn, her ponytail twisted into a sophisticated looking knot, shifted in her pew uneasily, but she threw Emily a friendly smile. Way in the back Lois Gordon sat in the corner of her pew. Her disapproving features looked like they were set in granite.

"Six years ago because of some foolish decisions I made, I found myself in one of the most difficult situations imaginable. I was an unmarried, pregnant teenager alone in Atlanta. I was running away from home, from God and from myself." Emily kept her fingers clamped on the polished wood of the podium. She recounted her downward spiral as concisely as she could, forcing herself not to make excuses for her behavior, which had included increasing bouts of shoplifting.

"At the time I didn't see what I was doing as wrong, although it obviously was. I was angry at the world because someone I trusted had disappointed me." She saw Lois Gordon shift irritably in her seat, but Emily tilted her chin up a notch and continued. "Being mad at the world was easier than being mad at myself. I thought other people owed me the things I needed, so when I could, I took them.

"One day I decided to shoplift at a pharmacy. I chose a little mom-and-pop-type store because I knew they wouldn't have the high-tech surveillance equipment that the chain stores always had."

Emily took a deep, shaky breath. "I was several months pregnant by then. I had started worrying that my baby wouldn't be healthy because I was eating only junk foods, so for the first time I decided to shoplift something that wasn't strictly just for me. I decided to steal some prenatal vitamins. That turned out to be both the worst and the best decision I'd ever made... because I got caught."

Abel had looked up from his hands, and his eyes were on her face, his expression unreadable. Emily's eyes found his, and as she continued she felt as if she were telling her story to him alone. "I'd never been arrested before, and I was terrified and angry and just an all-around hot mess. But that's when things started to change. The owner of the pharmacy, Mr. Arlowe, was a Christian, and the fact that I was trying to steal vitamins for my baby got his attention."

With her eyes fixed on Abel's face, Emily talked about how Mr. Arlowe had shown up in court and had petitioned the judge to remand her into a Christian home for single mothers. She described how the elderly man and his wife had visited her there, bringing her flowers and little items for the babies, and how this help coming in her darkest hour had finally opened her heart so that faith and hope came rushing in.

"So, I have to tell you that the stories you've been hearing about me are probably mostly true." She pulled her gaze away from Abel's face and looked back at the rest of the congregation. "I'm not asking you to trust me. You don't really know me, and I understand better than most that trust should be earned. I just want you to know that my story doesn't end back there in my darkest days. I want you to understand that if you or somebody you love is in a dark place like I was, your story doesn't have to end there, either."

She offered them a brief smile and then began to make her way back to her pew. A noise caught her attention, and when she glanced up she saw Abel. He was standing and clapping, his jaw set like a rock.

She stopped halfway to her seat, stunned. One by one several other people stood and joined in the applause. Emily gave the congregation a bewildered glance and then offered them all another grateful smile as she hurried over to the relative anonymity of her seat.

As she sidled past Abel, he reached out and took her forearm again, but this time his grip was gentle.

"You were right," he said under his breath. "You did need to do that."

Emily gave him a quick nod and hurriedly sat down next to Phoebe, who smiled up at her. "They liked you, Mama," she said in a stage whisper before holding up the bulletin she'd been scribbling on. "Look. I drawed a bird!"

"Thank you, Emily." Pastor Stone had reclaimed his pulpit, and he was beaming out over his congregation. "It's not often we have a standing ovation in church. That's unfortunate because we have a lot to clap about around here. Now, if you'll turn to page three hundred in your hymnal—"

"This," came a ringing voice from the back of the

Chapter Nine

Lois Gordon was standing up in the back of the church, and even from this distance, Abel could tell that the plump woman was shaking like a leaf in a thunderstorm.

"You had the gall to lecture me when all I was doing was protecting the businesses of this community, and then you turn around and give this *criminal* a job working for the church?"

"Miss Lois, this isn't the time." Stone spoke firmly from his pulpit, but the elderly lady wasn't about to let him get a word in edgewise.

"I can't think of a better one! Particularly if you still expect me to foot the bulk of the bill for the new fellowship hall." A murmur rippled through the congregation, and one of Lois's friends reached up a tentative hand to touch her elbow. Lois shrugged it off. "No, I'm not sitting down. I've had enough of this nonsense. But you—" the old lady turned her baleful gaze from the pastor to the people in the pews "—you have no more sense than to applaud such foolishness! For shame! If my husband were still alive and a deacon of this church, he'd never stand for this!"

She was most likely right about that. Abel figured Dr. Gordon would have shut this down in a wink. He and those like him were one reason Abel had steered clear of church for as long as he had.

"Let's go, Emily," Abel said quietly. He began to gather up the children's crayons and papers that were scattered over the pew. The wide-eyed twins helped him, darting uneasy glances toward the back of the sanctuary.

"No." Emily was sitting bolt upright in her seat. Those two telltale spots were burning high on her cheekbones, but the rest of her face was as white as paper. She kept her eyes fixed straight ahead. "I'm seeing this through."

Meanwhile, Lois Gordon's voice was growing louder and shriller. "You are *ruining* this church, Jacob Stone! First you waste our good money on that ridiculous coffee shop, and then you hire *her* to run it. If that's good stewardship of church funds, I'm a gardenia! That girl is a loose woman with a criminal history, and she has no business coming in the door of this church, much less working for it!"

"Miss Lois, I believe you've said just about enough," Jack Lifsey spoke up from his pew, and several other churchgoers nodded in agreement. "We're supposed to be Christians here."

"I'll let you know when I've said enough," the old lady retorted. "If the likes of Emily Elliott can get up and speak in this sanctuary, I certainly can!"

Stone had a quick aside with the music minister, who hurried to the pulpit as Stone started down the aisle.

From the set of the preacher's mouth, Abel figured he was planning to pry Lois Gordon out of her pew or die trying. Either way, Abel wanted Emily and the twins a safe distance away.

"Let's step outside, Emily. If you're set on staying till the end of service, we can come back in after Stone gets all this under control." If Stone could, which seemed unlikely at the moment. Abel watched as Lois snatched her arm away from the minister's gentle hand and refused to budge.

The murmuring in the pews increased. Nobody was paying much attention to the music minister's attempt to start the hymn. They were too focused on the drama unfolding at the back of the church, and they looked from Lois and the pastor back to Emily, whispering.

"Emily?" Abel prodded.

"No, I'm not leaving."

He saw Emily's neck pulse as she swallowed hard.

"But I'd really appreciate it if you'd take the children out for me. Please."

He opened his mouth to argue, but then Emily looked over at him. She was pale and shaking, but there was a determination in her eyes that made his protest stall in his throat.

"Please, Abel," she repeated quietly. "I can handle this."

He hesitated a minute, but he could see that she'd dug in her heels. Reluctantly he gave in, got up and shepherded the children out, cutting a wide berth around Lois, who was now surrounded by a wary circle of people, all trying to persuade her to leave the sanctuary. They didn't seem to be making much headway, because the old lady was well beyond the point of rea-

son. It looked like somebody was going to have to pick
her up and carry her out of the church. Abel was about
ready to volunteer for the job himself, and he knew a
thorny holly bush out on the front lawn of the church
that would make the perfect dropping-off point.

He looked back at Emily, who gave her confused
children a little wave and smiled brightly at them. Reassured, the twins went willingly through the door, but
Abel lingered for a second. Emily's smile had been big,
but it looked thin. He hated leaving her there sitting
alone in this mess, but as usual that was exactly what
she wanted him to do.

Once outside, he let the children play on the church's
playground while he worried over Emily and fought the
temptation to go back into the sanctuary. He leaned
against a handy oak and watched the children swinging on the swing set. They seemed happy enough, glad
like any children would be to be playing instead of sitting quiet in a church pew.

Phoebe dismounted her swing clumsily and went
sprawling, and Abel quickly pushed off the tree trunk
and started in her direction. Before he could make it to
her, her brother stopped to help her up, bending to brush
the bits of grass and dirt from the front of her dress and
checking her knees for scrapes. She must have passed
Paul's inspection, because a second later the two were
off and running to the big curving slide.

Abel's heart swelled with an unfamiliar pride. Emily
had done a great job with those two. They were good
kids, both of them. Any man would be proud to claim
them as his own.

He might as well be honest with himself. *He'd* be
proud to claim them.

That was something he'd never seen coming. His own dad sure hadn't been much of an advertisement for fatherhood. And Abel's struggling teenage attempts to take care of his headstrong younger brother had pretty much strangled any desire to have kids of his own.

But then Emily and her twins had come back to Goosefeather Farm, and something had shifted loose deep down inside him. New notions had been skirting around the edge of his mind for a while now, and those ideas had come front and center when he kissed Emily on the porch. Now they were all he could think about—though he could see his kiss had spooked her, and he knew he'd have to bide his time.

Abel's years around animals had taught him that rushing frightened creatures only made things worse. So he'd let Emily have her space even though the more she talked about working in that coffee shop Stone had dreamed up, the more uneasy Abel felt.

Jacob Stone was a solid man and a good preacher. He didn't trip over his own tongue, either, and the women sure seemed to like the look of him. Maybe Emily had Abel's mind twisted a bit sideways, but he still had enough sense to know that he was no competition for a man like Stone when it came to setting female hearts pattering. If he was as unselfish as he ought to be, he'd push Emily in Stone's direction and wish them both well, but the very thought of her and her children being claimed by another man, even a decent one like Stone, made Abel's stomach churn.

He heard a noise and glanced over toward the sidewalk that led to the church's rear parking lot. The sight he saw hit him like a punch.

Lois Gordon was being led to her car by one of her

cronies, Gayle Morris. Gayle had one arm protectively around her red-faced friend, who still looked fit to be tied.

"Can you believe this foolishness?" Lois was sputtering like an angry hen. "Asking me to leave. *Me!*"

Abel frowned. He'd better round up the twins and take them back to Emily before Lois saw them and started more trouble.

As it turned out, Lois wasn't the one he should have been worrying about.

Paul and Phoebe sprinted over and planted their little feet on the sidewalk in front of the two ladies. Abel had already started in their direction, but when he saw the look on Paul's face, he upgraded his walk to a trot.

"You were mean to my mother," Paul said in a clear, matter-of-fact tone. "You're not a nice lady." Phoebe stood a cautious foot or two behind her brother, but her face had the same accusing look to it. She nodded her agreement.

"Paul, Phoebe," Abel called out, trying a tone he'd found useful in dealing with balky animals. "We need to get on back into the church." Phoebe flicked an uncertain glance in his direction, but Paul kept his focus on the women in front of him.

"Go away, little boy!" Gayle darted a worried look at Lois's face and waved her hand in a shooing gesture. Lois's face had shifted from beet red to pasty white. She couldn't seem to take her eyes off Paul.

Paul favored Trey a good bit, especially around the eyes. Abel felt a flash of pity for the old woman, and when he reached the little group, he spoke more gently than he'd intended.

"Excuse us, Mrs. Gordon, Mrs. Morris. Phoebe, Paul, I said we need to go back inside the church now."

"No! Not yet. Wait." Lois Gordon never took her eyes off Paul's face. "Wait just a minute." She was breathing hard, and her friend clucked worriedly.

"Lois, honey, are you all right? You're a terrible color. Do you need to sit down?"

Lois clutched at her friend's arm. "You see it, don't you, Gayle? Anybody could see it! He's the spitting image. Just the spitting image!"

"Yes, honey. I see it." The other woman looked over at Abel, telegraphing her concern with her eyebrows. He nodded, but before he could speak Lois went on breathlessly.

"I never saw him up close before. And the girl." Lois moved her gaze over to Phoebe, who promptly took a step backward. "The resemblance isn't so striking, but I can see Trey in her, too. Don't you, Gayle?"

"Yes." Her friend nodded and patted Lois's arm. "I see it, Lois. Of course I do. But it's hot out here, honey, and I think we need to get you on home. You're terribly upset."

"Upset. Yes." Lois repeated her friend's words absently, her eyes moving from one twin to the other. Her reaction had flustered them, and they looked uneasily at Abel. He put his hands protectively on their shoulders, maneuvering them off the sidewalk and onto the grass beside him.

"Excuse us," Abel repeated, not bothering to put much warmth in his voice. He felt sorry for Lois Gordon, but his pity only went so far. "We'll let you ladies get on your way now."

Lois detached her gaze from the twins and looked

up into his face. The shock in her expression ebbed away, replaced by a chilly haughtiness. "Abel Whitlock," she said.

"Yes, ma'am." He met her eyes squarely. She didn't give an inch but met him stare for stare.

"My Trey never would say, but I know it was you who bloodied his nose all those years ago."

She had him there. "Trey and I had a difference of opinion that day, and I let my temper get the best of me." He didn't apologize. He still struggled with being sorry for that. Sometimes the line between Christian forgiveness and standing up for what was right seemed mighty blurry.

"He had to have plastic surgery, you know. We should have sent you the bill."

He didn't blink. "I'd have paid it and counted it a bargain. Ma'am."

Trey's mother sniffed scornfully. "You did it for *her*, I suppose. Because Trey wasn't fool enough to shipwreck his life and marry her. That girl always had you wrapped around her little finger, same as my Trey. Only she didn't give you the time of day, did she? She had her sights set higher back then." Those icy eyes measured him. "Small wonder. I knew your father. He was a good-for-nothing kind of a man. Your grandfather, too."

Abel remained silent, but he could feel a muscle twitching in his cheek. Lois's sharp eye saw it, and she permitted herself a small, satisfied smile.

"I don't like you, Whitlock, but I give credit where credit is due," the older woman continued smoothly. "I've always admired people who are able to pull themselves above the level of their raising. You've done that by all accounts, and so I'm going to give you a word of advice. Be very careful where you bestow your affections, or you'll sink right back down into the mess you came up from. A bad woman can ruin a good man."

"Are you calling my mama a bad woman?" Paul spoke up from Abel's side, and Abel could feel the tension in the boy's small shoulders. "She's not bad."

"Of course she isn't, Paul." Abel kept his eyes locked on Lois Gordon's. "I'm sure that's not what Mrs. Gordon meant. Now we'll need to go back into church, or your mama will be wondering what's happened to us." He dipped his head courteously toward the two women. "Ladies."

Gayle only blinked at him, but Lois responded with a curt nod of her own. He turned back toward the church with the children in tow.

"Mark my words," he heard Lois Gordon call behind him. "You think your daddy always had a drinking problem? He didn't, not until he took up with Gina Finch. The Whitlock men always choose the wrong women, and it's their ruination. Everybody knows that."

Abel set his jaw and kept walking. He had to give the woman credit. When it came to pushing people's buttons, she was a force to be reckoned with.

The service was over, and people were coming through the church's arched doorway in a steady stream. Abel stopped beside a large concrete planter full of begonias to wait for Emily. He couldn't help noticing that people didn't look nearly so uplifted as they usually did after one of Stone's sermons.

In fact, most of them looked a little shell-shocked. Jacob Stone definitely did. The pastor was dutifully manning his usual post by the front door, shaking hands and passing pleasantries, but from the look on his face, he needed a couple of aspirin and the afternoon off.

But Stone wasn't Abel's concern. Emily was. When he caught sight of her slender form coming out of the darkness of the church foyer, he zeroed in on her expression, trying to read it for clues.

She looked all right, he realized with some relief. The two red spots on her cheeks had faded into pink, and her chin was at its calmer angle. He could see why it was taking her so long to make it out of the church. Every few steps somebody else came up to hug her and whisper into her ear. Emily would be released by one person and would walk a few steps only to be stopped by somebody else.

As she neared him he saw her eyes dart to her children. A smile warmed her face, and she gave the twins a little wave. But before she could advance more than a couple of steps, Bailey Quinn stopped her with a hand on her arm.

Emily smiled, but Abel caught sight of the little signs of weariness on her face. She'd had enough. She was worn out, and she needed to go home. She was just too polite to say so.

Well, he wasn't. He crossed the distance between them in two easy strides, cupped one hand under Emily's elbow and crooked his best smile at the two women.

"Hate to interrupt your jawing, Bailey, but I'm thinking Emily needs to get her children on home now."

"Sure thing." Bailey flashed her dimples in his direction. Her dark eyes flicked between the two of them, and the corners of her mouth tipped up. "Well, well, well. I have to say I like the way this wind is blowing!

Now that you two are a couple, Abel, maybe you can talk Emily into staying in town."

Abel started to smile in return, but when he caught sight of Emily's expression, his face froze. Bailey's remark hadn't gone over well. Those two red spots were back, and her chin tilted up to its fighting angle.

"Abel and I aren't a couple. We're just friends." Emily flashed her friend a firm smile. "See you at the coffee shop on Friday. Okay?"

"Sure thing," Bailey repeated, her eyes telegraphing worried questions into Abel's. She was wasting her time. He was just as confused as she was.

"Sorry about that." Emily didn't meet his gaze as they walked back to the parking lot. "I forgot how bad small towns are. Everybody knows everybody's business, or they think they do."

"Didn't bother me," Abel responded easily, but he was troubled. Bailey's remark hadn't bothered him, but it had sure bothered Emily.

And that *had* bothered him.

The next Friday Emily sniffed the air at the Grounds of Faith Café suspiciously and bent over to peer into its unpredictable secondhand oven. She grabbed two pot holders and reached in to slide out the large muffin tin.

"Moment of truth here," she said over her shoulder to Bailey, who was busy labeling jars. Bailey leased the use of the café's commercial kitchen one day a week to process the canned goods she sold in her store. Today she'd been pressure canning spaghetti sauce, and the smell of the spiced tomatoes and peppers mingled with the aroma of fresh muffins.

"So?" Bailey paused in her labeling, raising a dark eyebrow. "Did you hit the sweet spot this time?"

Emily inspected her muffins anxiously, then relaxed with a smile. "Looks like it. I was right. This big stinker bakes about fifteen degrees too hot. I just need to reduce the temperature. That's a relief! You know how small towns are. One more batch of overbrowned scones, and my reputation as a baker would have been ruined forever."

Bailey walked over beside her, appropriated a hot muffin and took a careful bite. "Yum!" she said when she could talk. "I don't think you've got anything to worry about. At least..." She hesitated. "Not where your muffins are concerned."

Emily frowned. She thought she knew what Bailey was referring to, and that meant it was high time to change the direction of this conversation. "It's about time to open up," she said brightly.

"Yeah, I've got to go unlock my store." Bailey paused. Emily glanced at her, and her heart sank. Her old friend had a resolute expression on her face. "Listen, Emily, I'm sorry about making that comment at church. I mean, about you and Abel. I just assumed—"

"That's okay," Emily interrupted swiftly. "No harm done. Don't worry about it."

"Yeah." Bailey chewed on her lower lip for a second. "Don't be mad, but I need to say something. All right?"

Emily sighed. "Sure. Go ahead." She pulled on a pair of latex gloves and began arranging the muffins on a tray. "I'm listening."

"Be careful, Emily. I mean, it's probably no big deal. Abel's never been serious about a woman since I've known him. But there's always been something in the way he looks at you, even way back, and now… I don't know. Like I said, maybe it's nothing. But Abel's my friend, too, and he's already had plenty of trouble in his life. Just don't send him any mixed signals, okay?"

Emily nodded and managed a smile as Bailey picked up her box of jarred sauce and headed out the back door.

Mixed signals. Bailey's advice was coming a little too late. Emily's mind flashed back to Abel's kiss and her weak-kneed reaction to it, and the muffin she was holding slipped out of her suddenly clumsy fingers and tumbled across the stainless steel table.

Annoyed with herself she picked up the muffin and set it precisely on the tray. Then as she grabbed for a paper towel to wipe up the trail of crumbs it had left in its wake, she knocked the towels off the table, and they unrolled lavishly across the linoleum floor. She sighed deeply and began gathering them up.

This was ridiculous. Lately her brain was like one of those networks that showed marathons of the same movie over and over. She'd relived Abel's kiss half a million times since that afternoon, and every time she either dropped something or broke something. She was a grown woman. There was no reason for her to be this flustered over a kiss.

But Bailey had a point. Emily needed to be clear with Abel about this, and she would be…if he ever tried to kiss her again. He hadn't, not yet anyway. That was a good thing, of course, even if she did wonder just a tiny bit *why* he hadn't.

The little bell on the door jangled, and Emily tugged her apron straight, picked up the muffin tray and headed back out to the counter. She put a bright, welcoming smile on her face and pushed her thoughts about Abel Whitlock to the back of her mind.

A middle-aged couple was looking around the café with interest. As Emily came up behind the glass-fronted display counter, the pair glanced at each other and approached hesitantly.

Emily slid the heavy tray of muffins expertly into the display case and turned a reassuring smile on the couple. She'd helped dozens of newbie customers just like them back in Atlanta, and she figured they were feeling a bit bewildered by the assortment of coffees and flavors available.

As she began explaining the coffee menu, Emily felt the comfortable assurance of knowing exactly what to do. It was a welcome change from the bewilderment of trying to work the farm. Just yesterday afternoon, trying to prove that this job wasn't going to keep her from holding up her end of the farm chores, she'd picked a big basket of butter beans only to have Abel explain to her that they weren't quite ripe yet. Sure enough, when he'd slit open the pods, the little beans inside were barely formed. The goats had enjoyed them, but Emily had remembered the hot, backbreaking work of picking them, and she'd felt irked and stupid.

Here in the coffee shop it was different. Being here after struggling on the farm felt like slipping on her favorite pair of sneakers after a long day in heels. The sooner she returned to Atlanta and got back to restaurant work full-time, the better.

And that was just another reason why she had no business kissing Abel Whitlock.

"Mmm." The woman took a sip of her mocha latte and closed her eyes in ecstasy. "Herb, you don't know what you're missing. This is wonderful." Emily smiled. The lady had a sweet tooth and a weakness for chocolate. Emily had guessed right.

"You should try one of these muffins, Marjorie. In fact, we should get some to take home." Herb, who had stubbornly clung to black coffee without frills, was halfway through one of Emily's supersized cranberry almond muffins, and he looked just as happy as his wife. Emily's smile widened. These two would be back. She'd just created two more regulars for Grounds for Faith.

Just as Emily turned back to tinker with the temperamental milk steamer, the bell jangled again. She spoke up cheerfully over her shoulder. "Welcome to Grounds of Faith!"

"Try the muffins," Herb volunteered with his mouth full. "They're amazing."

"They always are," drawled a familiar voice. Emily turned to find Abel giving her his crooked smile. Her heart did its usual foolish little leap in response.

Stop that, she warned herself firmly.

"Cranberry almond or chocolate walnut?" she asked him, using her best professional voice.

"Too tough to decide. I'll take one of each and a cup of black coffee. Please."

"I didn't know there were chocolate muffins, too," Herb said, his eyes on the plate Emily was preparing for Abel. "I'll try one of those. Hush, Marjorie. I'm having one, I said. We'll eat salads for supper."

Emily set another chocolate muffin on a fresh plate and handed it over the counter to Herb, who sighed happily as he took a generous bite. When he could speak again, he nodded at Abel. "You'd better hang on to this one, Whitlock. Not only is she pretty as a picture, but she can really cook, too."

Emily flushed and shot an uncomfortable look in Abel's direction. "Oh, but we're not—" she began, but Abel reached across the counter and covered her hand with the rough warmth of his own.

"You're a mighty smart man, Mr. Austin," he said, his blue eyes holding Emily's. His thumb stroked the back of her hand gently, and Emily's butterflies reacted as if they'd just been given a round of espressos. She could feel the color flaming up in her cheeks, but somehow she couldn't detach her gaze from Abel's.

Dimly she heard Herb chuckling and Marjorie fussing. "Stop teasing them, Herb. You're embarrassing her. Come on. Let's go sit by the window and leave the sweethearts in peace."

Mixed signals. Bailey's voice echoed in Emily's mind, and she jerked her hand away belatedly. "What are you doing in town?" she asked, busying herself with ringing up the sale.

"The part for the tractor came, and I drove in to pick it up." From the corner of her eye she watched as Abel settled himself on the stool at the counter. "While I was here I thought I'd stop in and see how you were getting along. Maybe take a look at that oven that's been giving you trouble."

"Thanks, but you don't have to do that."

"I don't mind." Abel set down his coffee mug and got to his feet. "Matter of fact, why don't I go on back to the kitchen and—"

"No!" Emily spoke sharply. She glanced at the Austins, who were lingering over their muffins at a cor-

ner table, and lowered her voice. "I figured it out this morning."

"All right." Abel sank back down on his stool and raised his coffee mug to his lips, his blue eyes watching her warily over its rim.

"We enjoyed it, girlie," Herb called as he and Marjorie rose to deposit their trash in the bin. "We'll be back soon. You can count on that! Mind what I told you, Whitlock. If you have any sense, you'll hang on to this one!"

Abel chuckled and waved as the couple ambled outside. "Herb Austin's one of the biggest gossips in Pine Valley, Emily. He'll tell everybody in town about your muffins. They'll be beating down the door in the morning."

"That's probably not all he'll be telling, either," Emily muttered. She put down the cloth she'd been using to wipe off the counter and looked Abel squarely in the eye. "You heard them. They think we're sweethearts. And you're encouraging it."

There was a beat of silence. Abel gently placed his half-eaten muffin on his plate. "And that bothered you."

"I don't want people around here thinking we're a couple."

"Ah." Something shifted slightly in his expression, hardening it. "Worried about your reputation?"

Disbelief flashed through her. "Are you trying to be funny? You know as well as I do what my reputation is in this town. No matter what I've done or how I've changed, I'll always be the girl who got herself in trouble with Trey Gordon. But I certainly never thought you'd be the one to cast it up to me!" She turned to go back into the sanctuary of the café kitchen, but he reached out fast and took hold of her wrist.

"Whoa! You're shoveling some pretty hard words in my mouth, Emily, and I sure don't need that. We both know I talk myself into enough trouble without any help. Maybe I'm not so good at making myself clear, but you ought to know me well enough to give me the benefit of the doubt. You know that's not what I meant, and after church last Sunday you ought to know that's not what other folks think, either."

The gentle pressure of his fingers on her arm made her throat go suddenly dry. "What did you mean, then?"

"I was talking about me. Who I am. My family isn't exactly known for boosting folks' reputations."

Emily swallowed and pulled her arm away. "You should take a dose of that medicine you're so busy dishing out. You ought to know *me* well enough to know I'd never think such a thing, Abel Whitlock. Your last name has nothing to do with this, and you should really consider taking that chip off your shoulder. You've already proven that you're not like the rest of your family, ten times over. Everybody knows it but you."

There was a pause as they stared at each other over the counter. Abel took a slow breath. "All right. Now that we've got that settled, I reckon we might as well get the rest of it out in the open. We both know what the real trouble is. You've been as nervous as a cat with nine tails ever since I kissed you."

At his words, the memory of it flashed through her mind, and she jumped, knocking over the napkin dispenser. She righted it with shaking fingers, swallowed and tilted up her chin. He was right. They might as well meet this head-on and get it over with. "That kiss should never have happened."

"You think so?" He raised his eyebrows at her. "Looks like I'm about as bad at kissing as I am at talking."

"That's not what I meant! You're very good at... I mean, it was..." Emily stopped and flushed. "That's not the problem."

"What *is* the problem?"

"Well..." Emily picked up her rag and scrubbed hard at the countertop, avoiding his eyes. "For one thing, I'm only here temporarily. I'm moving back to Atlanta as soon as the summer's over, and you...well, you've got no plans to leave Pine Valley. Do you?"

"No. I can't say that I have."

"See? That's what I mean. You're the kind of man who stays put."

"That's true enough, I suppose."

"And I have the twins to consider. I can't afford to go chasing after every man I feel an attraction to. I made a decision a long time ago that I wasn't going to be like..." She trailed off. No point in bringing her mother into this. She started again. "I made a decision that I wasn't going to bring men in and out of my children's lives. I know firsthand what that's like, and I won't put the twins through it."

He nodded slowly. "I can see the rights of that. I surely can."

"Good." Emily blinked, feeling slightly taken aback by his easy agreement. She ignored an illogical flare of disappointment and nodded. "I'm glad you understand."

"I think I do." Abel got to his feet, placing his napkin neatly over his half-eaten breakfast and pulling money out of his wallet. "And it looks like I owe you an apology." She opened her mouth to protest, but he went on. "That kiss was a long time coming for me, Emily, but it looks like maybe it was too quick for you. I'm sorry about that."

What did he mean *a long time coming*? Emily shook her head. "No apology necessary, Abel. It was just a mistake, that's all."

"That what you're calling it?" The corner of Abel's mouth quirked up slightly. "Sweetest mistake I've ever made, then, and one I sure won't mind making again sometime when you're ready."

Emily felt her heartbeat quicken at the promise in his words, but she shook her head. "You're not listening to me," she began.

"Oh, I'm listening. When you're as bad at talking as I am, you get mighty good at listening. And what I'm hearing you say is that you're feeling the spark that's between us same as I am, and it's scaring you out of your mind. I understand that, and you can rest easy. I won't be rushing you. But I'm not going anywhere, either, not until we get this sorted out between us. It's like you said." The tilt at the corner of his mouth spread into an easy smile. "I'm the kind of man who stays put."

Chapter Ten

Abel finally maneuvered the agitated Jersey into her stand and clipped her halter to its front hook. "There you go, you stubborn old bovine," he muttered under his breath. The hardest part of his job was done, and he was glad Tim Anderson had to deal with the rest of it. Just in time, too. He could hear Anderson's truck rumbling up the driveway.

"That was quite a show!" Emily observed nervously. She and the twins had been watching him tussle with the rampaging cow from the far corner of the barn.

"It always is." Abel paused and wiped the sweat off his forehead with the sleeve of his cotton shirt. "Beulah's not exactly a fan of the artificial insemination process, and somehow she always knows what we're up to." He smiled at the twins. "But next spring we'll have a pretty new calf and lots of fresh milk, so it's all worth it."

Emily cleared her throat. "Being bred makes her worth more, right? Remember, we'll be selling her at the end of the summer."

Emily's words jabbed at him, and he felt a wave of

irritation. Ever since their talk at the coffee shop, she'd been using every opportunity that came her way to remind him that she and the twins would be leaving the farm as soon as they could. As usual, he'd somehow managed to say the wrong thing. She was well and truly spooked now, and it was all his fault.

Today she looked even more tense than usual. She'd been that way ever since she found out that Tim Anderson was not only Miss Sadie's go-to guy for cow breeding but the county extension agent, as well.

Anderson came into the barn at a trot, both hands clutching the metal tackle box he used to carry his equipment. Glory was running behind him with her wings outstretched, honking nasally.

"Get on, goose! I'm telling you, Abel, that bird knows my truck. Every single time I've been out here, she's been waiting for me in the driveway." The county agent wiped his ruddy face while Glory hissed at him from the barn doorway. He set down his box, ran Beulah over with a practiced eye and nodded. "Looks like you've timed it just about right, Abel, as usual."

"Not hard to do," Abel replied easily. "Beulah always lets us know when she's ready for a new calf."

"She's a good old girl." Anderson slapped Beulah on the rump affectionately and then began to pull on his long rubber glove. "I sure was sorry to hear about Miss Sadie's passing. Even sorrier when I heard I was the one supposed to come out and check on how her granddaughter's running the farm. Didn't see anything amiss outside, but I expect she has you to thank for that. She's a city girl, I hear."

Abel shot a glance in Emily's direction. Anderson

hadn't seen her standing in the shadows with the twins. Before Abel could point her out, Anderson continued.

"They tell me she caused a big ruckus in the Pine Valley Church last Sunday. It looks like the preacher may lose his job over it, and that's a shame for sure."

"What are you going to do to our cow?" Paul came out of his corner, his small face creased with worry as he regarded the shoulder-length rubber glove on Anderson's right arm. "You're not going to hurt her, are you?"

Anderson jumped and spilled the contents of his tackle box across the barn floor. "Well, little man, you came out of nowhere, didn't you?" The man nodded in Emily's direction, looking embarrassed. "Ma'am," he said politely before turning his attention back to Paul. "Naw, I'm not going to hurt her. I'm going to help Beulah here make you a pretty new calf in about nine months. How does that sound?"

Emily had followed Paul out of the shadows and into the square of sunlight streaming through the barn door. "What did you mean when you said that Pastor Stone might lose his job?"

Anderson coughed. He leaned over and began gathering his equipment. "I was speaking out of turn, ma'am. I shouldn't be spreading gossip."

"But that's what you've heard?" Emily pressed her point, her gray-green eyes fixed on the man's ruddy face. "That his job is on the line over what happened on Sunday?"

Anderson cast a worried glance at Abel, but Abel offered him no help. "Aw, well. I wouldn't worry about it, ma'am. It probably won't come to anything. The church board's been a little agitated ever since Stone spearheaded that whole coffee shop thing, but everybody knows that they're not going to have an easy time find-ing another preacher half as good. They'll probably just yowl at him a little and then let it blow over."

Anderson began to prep his equipment, looking grateful for the distraction of his work. Abel's eyes met Emily's, and he knew they were both thinking the same thing. *Lois Gordon wouldn't let this blow over. Not in a million years.*

Anderson quickly finished his job and got back into his truck, leaving an irritated cow and two disgusted twins in his wake.

"That was icky!" Phoebe said, wrinkling her nose. Paul nodded his agreement.

Abel chuckled as he put the soiled rubber glove and the empty breeding straw in the trash bag he'd had ready. "Worth it, though," he said cheerfully. "Jersey calves are the prettiest little things you've ever seen, all big brown eyes and knock-knees. Just wait until spring-time. You'll see."

"We won't be here in the spring, remember?" Emily's voice had an edge to it. "In fact," she muttered under her breath, "considering the amount of trouble I'm caus-ing, I'm starting to wonder if we should be here now."

"Paul, why don't you and Phoebe go out and see if the plums are ripe yet? Pick a couple and bring them here for me to check. All right?"

"Sure! Come on, Pheebs." The twins scampered out the wide door into the sunshine, and Abel turned his attention back to their mother.

"Emily, if Stone's got a problem with his church board, that's not your fault."

She blew out a heavy sigh and shook her head. "If it weren't for me, none of this would have happened."

"I think you're wrong. Lois Gordon's been like a powder keg for years now, ever since Trey died. If you hadn't set her off, something else would have."

"Maybe so, but I sure wish I hadn't been the one to strike the match." Emily frowned and rubbed her face with her hand. She left a smudge of dirt across her cheek in the process. "I hate to think that Pastor Stone might lose his job just because he took my side."

"Stone doesn't strike me as the kind of guy who takes sides. He just does what he thinks is right."

"That's exactly why I don't want to be any part of him leaving Pine Valley Church." Emily scrubbed at her face again, leaving another smear of dirt across her forehead. Abel considered telling her, but he thought she looked cuter dirty than most women looked clean. "I can't let this happen. I've got to fix it if I can." She swallowed hard as he took a step toward her.

"Emily," he began, but she shook her head and waved him off.

"I'm going to clean up and go into town. I need to see if there's anything I can do about this. I'll quit the job at the coffee shop if I have to. Can you watch the twins for me? Please?"

"Sure. But—" he tried again.

"I won't be gone long," she said, and left the barn without meeting his eyes. Feeling uneasy, Abel watched her go.

He didn't like the direction Emily's thoughts were taking, not one bit. Not only didn't he like how Emily was clinging so stubbornly to her plan to leave Pine Valley, he wasn't crazy about her being so gung ho to rescue Jacob Stone from the clutches of his church board, either.

He heard the excited voices of the children, and through the barn doorway he could see them headed his way with their hands dripping full of ripe plums. Their faces lit up as they saw him waiting for them, and Phoebe waved happily, dropping several of her plums on the ground.

In spite of his worry, Abel found himself grinning as the twins halted and tried to scrabble up the plums Phoebe had dropped without losing the ones still in their hands. It was tough going, but they were laughing as they chased the rolling plums across the barnyard.

His heart swelled up and filled with a new determination. He'd meant what he'd said to Emily back in the coffee shop. That kiss had settled it as far as he was concerned. He'd set his heart on Emily Elliott, and he was staying put.

Now he just had to convince her to stick around, too. Somehow he had to find a way to help Emily see how happy she and her twins could be on Goosefeather Farm.

With him.

"Nope, I'm not letting you quit." Jacob Stone had plenty of charm, but during the course of the last twenty minutes, Emily had discovered that he also had a steel-plated backbone. "The coffee shop needs you."

She blew out an exasperated breath and frowned at the man seated behind the big varnished desk in the church office. "You could lose your job."

The pastor laughed. "Maybe."

"I can't let that happen!"

Jacob Stone laughed again. "You're not in charge of it. And neither am I. I work for God, Emily, before I work for any church. He'll let me know when I'm done here. In the meantime I'm going to do what He calls me to do, church board or no church board."

"Lois Gordon," Emily began, but the pastor waved his hand dismissively.

"Miss Lois doesn't run this church no matter what she may believe to the contrary, bless her heart." Stone got out from behind his desk and walked over to Emily with his hand extended. "I appreciate your concern. I truly do. But don't waste your time worrying about me."

Emily sighed and stood up. She accepted the handshake and conceded defeat. "You know, I'm starting to see why your church board finds you so frustrating."

"Keep them in your prayers. They need all the help they can get, believe me." He walked with her to the office door. "I'm hearing great things about your muffin ministry, by the way. It looks like you're a hit."

Muffin ministry. Emily chuckled. "Once I finally quit burning everything, business really seemed to take off. I've had to start tripling my batches."

"And you came in here to talk about quitting? Let me give you a word of advice, Emily. Never, ever give up on what the Lord is blessing, no matter how crazy it may seem. God often leads us into unexpected places, and if we've got the courage to follow Him, it always pays off. Save me a muffin tomorrow morning, okay? Something with chocolate."

As she drove back to the farm, Emily reflected on Jacob Stone's words. She was still pondering the idea of following God into unexpected places when her cell phone trilled.

"I've been sitting still on Spaghetti Junction for forty-five minutes." Clary's irritated voice came through the speakerphone. "And I'm bored to death. This Atlanta traffic is enough to make me want to move to a small town like Pine Valley and take up knitting. Talk me out of it."

"You called at the wrong time for that, Clary. I'm likelier to talk you into it. I could sure use a friend down here right now."

"Oh? What's going on?"

Emily filled Clary in on the debacle with Lois Gordon and her recent conversation with Jacob Stone.

"Good for him," Clary said. "He's not going to let that Lois bully him. I like his style. Well, I've only moved about three feet forward, so what else you got?"

Something about her friend's familiar voice broke down Emily's reserves, and she found herself telling Clary all about her dilemma with Abel.

"Now, that *is* interesting. You sure know how to perk up a traffic jam." Emily's friend's chuckle floated through the speaker. "I can't believe it! You haven't even been out in the country for three months, and you're already falling in love!"

Emily felt her heart skip a beat. "Don't be ridiculous."

"I know you, Emily Elliott, and you don't kiss recreationally. It sounds to me like this man's got something breaking loose in that armor-plated heart of yours, and high time, too!"

"You're blowing this all out of proportion, Clary. It was one kiss, and it's not happening again. I'm not ready for a relationship right now."

Clary sighed. "I've heard that before. You aren't ready now, you weren't ready last year and you probably won't be ready next year, either. 'I'm not ready' is just an excuse, Emily, and it's not even a very good one. I should know. I tried it on my mom the first day of kindergarten. She made me go anyway."

"Well, at least you had a mom who cared if you went to kindergarten. The truant officer had to show up before my mother even remembered I was supposed to start school. She was distracted by the Australian tennis pro who was the flavor of the month just then. I'm not going to be like her, Clary. I'm just not."

"I don't think being attracted to a decent man means you're a bad mother. Anyway, you couldn't be like Marlene if you tried, hon."

"Oh, yes, I can. The twins are proof of that."

"That," Clary said quietly, "was a long time ago, Emily. You've changed."

"And I don't have any plans to change back. I know you mean well, Clary, but you're going to have to trust me on this. I need to keep my focus where it belongs. There's no room in my life for romance right now."

Especially not with a man who affected her judgment the way Abel did. Emily disconnected the call and made the final turn down the bumpy road that led to the farm. Everything about the man set her nerves jangling; she was on high alert every time she was with him. She noticed every smile and every expression. She knew the way his muscles shaped the sleeves of his shirt when he tossed hay bales out of the back of his pickup as if they were made of cotton candy. And the watchful, protective affection he had for the twins could warm her heart to its melting point in a split second.

She found being around Abel unsettling and exhilarating, which was pretty much the way she'd felt six years ago around Trey Gordon. She was older and wiser now, and she had the anchor of her faith and her beloved twins to steady her. Yet in spite of all that, she was puddling like hot butter every time Abel Whitlock looked at her. It made no sense.

No matter what Clary said, Emily knew she was backsliding. She was acting just like her mother. When it came to men, Marlene Elliott never made sense, either.

Emily turned into the gravel driveway and stopped the car. She rolled down her balky window to retrieve the mail from the battered mailbox, proud that she'd actually remembered to do so. It was another aspect of country living she'd had to get used to. If she didn't think to grab the mail on her way in or out, it meant a special trek down the long, winding driveway to get it.

Waves of heat radiated off the asphalt through her open window, but it was too hard to manhandle the thing back up, so she left it down as she flipped through the envelopes. Suddenly she froze, her hand on the church's weekly newsletter. Something was wrong.

The ordinary noises of birds singing and bugs chirring still rose from the hot grass, but there was another sound in the mix now, a high-pitched, excited sound.

Somebody was screaming.

Emily threw her car into Drive and stomped on the accelerator. Her tires spun in the gravel as she sped toward the farmhouse.

Chapter Eleven

Emily's heart was halfway up her throat and pulsing like a jackhammer by the time she rounded the last curve and caught sight of the house.

Her children and that annoying goose were in the west pasture under the plum trees. Both Phoebe and the normally unflappable Paul were running around in circles yelling while Glory stood her ground with her neck and wings extended, honking for all she was worth. For a second Emily thought the twins had been stung by some of the yellow jackets that tended to cluster on the fallen plums. Then Abel came out of the barn, and she understood exactly what was provoking the screams and the nasal honking.

He was leading a saddled horse by the reins.

Emily blinked. There had never been a horse on Goosefeather Farm. Her grandmother hadn't been a fan of horses. She claimed that the animals ruined pastures and were too expensive to feed and look after.

She knew her kids had been disappointed that there was no horse on the farm. She also knew that horses were large animals who required expert handling and who could easily land a five-year-old in the hospital. What she didn't know was why there was a glossy chestnut horse walking out of her barn with a saddle on, twitching its black mane as it bobbed its head up and down in time with its steps.

The twins saw her approaching and abandoned their gleeful hopping to race in her direction. They flung their arms around her waist so exuberantly that she staggered.

"Look! Look, Mama! Mr. Abel got us a horsie!" Overcome with excitement, Phoebe was barely coherent.

"It's a *real* horse, Mama." Paul's arms were just as tight around her, and for once he was almost as breathless as Phoebe. "Not a pony. Mr. Abel says ponies are too can-tank-erous." Paul pronounced the new word with pride. "They're not as safe."

"'Cause they're little," Phoebe put in, "and being little makes them scared."

"Like how bantam roosters like Newman are usually meaner than the big roosters," Paul continued. Emily blinked. When had her son learned that? "She's a mare, Mr. Abel says. That means a girl."

"'Cause girls are *best*!" Phoebe released her mother, wrapped her arms around herself and resumed jumping up and down as Abel walked the horse over from the barn.

"They are not." For once Paul's heart wasn't in this particular argument. "Can I ride first, please, Mr. Abel?"

Abel crooked a smile at the boy and waited. Emily frowned as she watched her son's face change from hopeful expectation to resignation.

"I know, I know. Ladies first." Paul kicked at a clump of grass with one foot. "But are you sure that goes for sisters, too?"

"I'm positive, son. Tell you what. You let Phoebe be a lady and ride first, and I'll let you have an extra five minutes on your turn. How about that?"

"Wait a minute," Emily interjected desperately. "We need to talk about this."

"It's okay, Mama," Paul said with a hefty sigh. "Mr. Abel explained it. Letting girls go first is part of being a man. Even if they aren't really ladies, just sisters. It still counts. Right?" As Emily watched, her son looked up into Abel's face for affirmation.

He got it. "Right." Abel reached out with his free hand and tousled her son's blond hair in a fatherly gesture.

That did it.

"Nobody's riding anything," Emily said tightly.

"Mama!" Aghast, the twins stared at her.

"I'm sorry, but my answer is no. Not," she pointed out, "that I was ever actually asked a question. Neither of you has a helmet to wear, and Phoebe's wearing sandals. I don't know much about horses, but even I know enough to know that you need boots and helmets to ride safely."

"But Mr. Abel was just going to lead us around the pasture. He won't let us fall off. Can't we ride the horse, Mama? Please?" Paul sounded about two seconds away from tears, and he was the twin who rarely cried. Emily felt even worse.

"And I'll go into the house fast as fast and put on my tennis shoes, Mama! Paul can ride first while I do that. I'll let him be the lady this time. Okay?" Phoebe put her hands together and turned the full force of her pleading eyes on her mother. "Please?"

"Molly here's a gentle, middle-aged girl, Emily," Abel inserted quickly. "She's good with children and used to them. That's why I chose her. I'll walk 'em slow and just around the field this time. I'll pick up some helmets this afternoon when I go into town."

"Boots, too?" Paul asked worriedly. "Mama said boots."

Abel nodded. "Boots, too."

"I want purple ones!" Phoebe resumed bouncing.

"Nobody is riding this horse," Emily repeated. "And good boots and helmets are expensive. We can't afford that right now."

"My treat," Abel said quickly, and Emily shot him a look that made the smile die out of his eyes.

"No, thank you. Kids, go in the house, please."

"But, Mama—" Paul began desperately as Phoebe burst into dramatic tears.

"Mind your mother," Abel said quietly. "We kind of sprang this whole thing on her, and she doesn't know what to think about it. That's my fault."

"Go to the house. I'll be up in a minute. Watch some cartoons," Emily suggested recklessly. The children took one look at her face, read her expression and gave up. They trudged off across the pasture toward the white farmhouse with bowed heads. Phoebe was still sobbing, and Glory followed along behind them honking worriedly, her wings outspread.

"Emily," Abel began when the kids were out of earshot, but Emily cut him off.

"Where do you get off buying my kids a horse without checking with me first? What on earth were you thinking?"

There was a beat of silence. The bridle jangled as the mare shook her head and cocked a wary ear in Emily's direction. Abel stood like a statue with the leather reins looped loosely in one hand. His expression was tense, and his eyes searched Emily's face.

"It looks like I crossed a line somewhere," he said finally. "I'm sorry. The kids have been talking about horses ever since they got here, and I've had my eye out for one that might suit. When I heard about the Johnsons selling Molly here, I figured she'd be perfect. I told them to bring her on over."

"Without bothering to check it with me."

Another beat of silence. Molly stomped a hoof to displace a stinging fly. "I didn't mean anything in particular by keeping it quiet. I just… I wanted to surprise you and the kids."

"Let me make something very clear, Abel. When it comes to my children, I don't like surprises. What would have happened if I hadn't shown up when I did? You were going to let them ride this animal without my permission or knowledge and without boots or helmets. What if they'd been bucked off?"

Something flickered in Abel's stunned eyes. "Molly's never bucked anybody off in her life. She's as gentle as a tabby cat. Anyway, you don't think I'd put those kids on any horse likely to hurt them, do you? I told you once before that they won't come to any harm when they're with me. I gave you my word on it."

"Well, letting my kids ride a horse without any safety equipment in open-toed shoes is a pretty strange way to keep that word, don't you think?"

Abel drew in a slow breath and nodded. "I didn't notice Phoebe's shoes. I should have, though. You're exactly right about that. Truth is she shouldn't be wearing sandals anywhere in the pastures, whether she's riding or not. Hooves are sharp. Even a goat can step on a foot and cut it bad enough to need stitches. And then you've got the fire ants and yellow jackets to look out for, too. Paul and Phoebe both need boots. I'll see to it. I don't know if the store in town has purple ones, but hopefully I can find some that'll suit Phoebe well enough." He smiled that tantalizing crooked smile at her again, and Emily's heart did its customary dip and flip.

More than anything she wanted to smile back at him. She wanted to let this argument pass and let this man buy her children boots and horses and whatever else he wanted to buy them. She wanted to let him kiss her again until all the worries that kept her up at night just dissolved into nothingness. She wanted all that so badly she was shaking, and the strength of her longing terrified her.

She felt a surge of desperation. She had to draw the line right here and right now, or she'd never draw it at all.

"You're not buying my children boots." Her voice sounded strange to her own ears, sharp and cold, and Abel's warm smile faded. "Or a horse. Or anything else."

"Emily, what's going on?" Abel took a step toward her, and she backed up. She had to keep her distance. She couldn't afford to go all fuzzy like she always did when Abel was close to her. She had to keep what was left of her wits about her.

"No," she said thickly. It was all she could manage, but it did the job. He stopped where he was.

"Emily," Abel began again, and she could see the concern and confusion on his face. "Listen to me. I'm sorry I've got you all upset. I sure didn't mean to. All I wanted to do was—"

"I don't care what you wanted to do! For heaven's sake, who buys kids a horse without checking it out first with their mother? It's not like buying them a candy bar! A horse is a big deal! And what am I going to do when it's time to sell everything and go back to Atlanta? How are the kids going to feel then? They're already going to have to leave those chicks and…other things they've gotten attached to. It's going to be hard enough without adding more to it."

Abel kept his eyes on hers, his face tense and still. He nodded slowly. "You have a point there. If you're still set on leaving at the end of the summer, I reckon the horse could be a problem."

"What do you mean *if*? Of course I'm leaving!" Wasn't she? Of course she was. There was no question about it. This was all just temporary. Her life, her real life, was in Atlanta, not here with geese and goats and cows and men who bought your five-year-olds horses. "I've been telling you that all along."

A silence stretched between them, filled only by the soft snorts of the patient horse beside them, the buzz of the insects hidden in the pasture grass and the distant honking of Glory. She'd been left on the back step and was complaining about it. Abel just kept looking at Emily, his face unreadable.

Emily was trembling. She was on the edge of bursting into tears just like Phoebe, but she plunged ahead.

She wanted to get this straight. She needed everybody on the same page here. "The point I'm making is that it's not your *place*, Abel. It's not your place to buy my kids horses or boots or riding helmets. And incidentally it's certainly not your place to teach my son manners. One stupid kiss doesn't make us a couple, Abel. We're *friends*. That's it. I'm not looking for more than that, not with you or with any other man for that matter. And if I were, I wouldn't be looking in a place like Pine Valley."

The horse nickered uneasily beside them, and Abel soothed her automatically without taking his eyes off Emily.

She couldn't quite get her breath. This was all too much for her to deal with, too much to feel. She didn't *need* all this in her life. She couldn't handle it. She'd never been able to handle it, just like her mother. But she wasn't going to make the same mistakes Marlene had made. She just wasn't.

"All right." Abel's voice sounded oddly tight, and he looked as if he'd been slapped. "You've had your say, and you've made your point. All I can do is say I'm sorry for my misstep."

His tone was carefully polite, but the pain underneath it cut at her. She hated that she'd hurt him, but she had to put a stop to all this craziness once and for all. So she spoke again, softly but firmly.

"You're not their father, Abel. Please stop trying to act like one."

He said nothing. She'd seen Abel Whitlock at a loss for words a thousand times before, but never quite like this.

He nodded without meeting her eyes. Then he turned and began to walk the horse back toward the barn.

She lingered in the pasture watching him go. There had been a finality to that curt nod. She still wasn't sure exactly what had been blooming between them, but whatever it was, it was definitely over now.

And that was for the best. Emily swallowed hard and headed to the farmhouse. Hot tears blurred her vision, and she once again stumbled over the tough clumps of grass in the path.

This time, though, nobody was there to steady her.

Out in Mrs. Sadie's vegetable garden, Abel ruffled the soft green leaves of the last plant in the row, easily finding the cluster of slim beans dangling underneath them. He snapped them upward off their stems and tossed them into the brimming plastic bucket beside him before standing and straightening his aching back. He'd been working in the garden ever since he finished with the barn chores just after dawn. He was tired and sore from bending over, but hard physical work always cleared his mind, and he'd been sorely in need of that.

The refreshing coolness of the July morning had given way to the muggy heat of a Georgia summer day, and he was drenched with sweat and thirsty. But the garden was picked and weeded clean, and the animals were fed. Beulah was milked, and her barn had been mucked out and spread with clean straw. Goosefeather Farm had a contented, well-tended air about it. That gave him a small sense of satisfaction, and nowadays he was finding satisfaction pretty hard to come by.

But now his work here was done. Whether he liked it or not, it was time to go home and either wander around his workshop or go stir-crazy in his cabin. He didn't seem to be able to do much else these days.

Abel hefted the two buckets that were brimming with green beans, squash and tomatoes and started back toward the farmhouse. He would set them on the screened porch, poke his head in the door and let Emily know he was gone until the evening.

That had been his routine ever since the blowup about the horse. He and Emily had been circling around each other like two unacquainted cats. When they'd spoken, it had been about the farm work, nothing else, and they were both painfully polite. The chilly silence was driving Abel crazy, but he couldn't think of a way to fix it. He'd been spending some sleepless nights mulling it over as he carved in his workshop.

He'd already finished enough pieces to keep most of the shops on his roster supplied for a month or two. They were what he called filler pieces, simple carvings that were easy and mindless to make. They weren't particularly satisfying to carve, and once he finished them he chucked them in a box and never glanced at them again. Unfortunately they seemed to be all he was capable of making at the moment.

For once in his life, his heart wasn't in his carving. His workshop had always been the one place he felt whole and peaceful, and he'd always relished the solitude he'd had there.

That had all changed. Now as soon as he finished a carving, he found himself wanting to show it to Emily and the twins. He wanted to hear that soft awe in her voice as she turned the piece over in her hands and traced the grain of the wood with her finger. He wanted to hear Paul's and Phoebe's squeals of delight. His own approval had been all he'd ever needed for his work, but now it didn't feel like enough.

He was miserable. And what was worse, he had nobody to blame for it but himself.

Emily was right about the whole horse thing. He'd overstepped and pushed in where he hadn't been invited. That was the kind of thing that happened when a man let his dreams get the best of his common sense.

As long as he could remember, he'd dreamed about having what he'd experienced sitting at Emily Elliott's supper table. And ever since Danny left and Miss Sadie passed on, Abel's hunger for family had sharpened considerably. The time he'd spent with Emily and the little ones had whetted that appetite even more.

It was a hard thing to be given a taste of something you'd been hankering after all your life. It made a man reckless. That was the only excuse Abel could come up with for the way he'd acted. He'd grabbed with both hands for something that wasn't his, and he'd gotten smacked for it. He figured it served him right, but that didn't make it hurt less.

As he neared the farmhouse, Glory popped out from her hiding place in the moist bed of spearmint beside the back porch and honked loudly at him, jolting him out of his thoughts.

"Yes, I see you, and no, I haven't forgotten your treat," Abel told her as the goose extended her long neck in his direction, swiveling her head up to glare at him with one beady eye. He set his buckets down and reached into his pocket for the handful of sweet feed he always tucked in there. He sprinkled it in front of the goose, who gobbled it up as fast as it hit the ground.

"You're making her worse." Emily spoke from above him, and he glanced up to see her standing on the small screened back porch, considering the goose with a rueful expression. "And so are the twins. They come out here and feed her their bread crusts every time they can. She's taken to hanging around in that mint bed so much that she always smells like chewing gum." Her voice actually sounded affectionate, and Abel felt a stupid little flare of hope. If Glory was growing on her, maybe in time she'd start to see other things a little differently, too.

He tamped his feelings down firmly and tried to get a grip on himself. He was reading a lot into a greedy, mint-scented goose. That just showed how desperate he was, and desperation made people stupid. He'd just about had his fill of stupid.

"I'm done in the garden for now," Abel said, hefting up the full buckets again. "I'll just set these vegetables on the porch for you before I go. Bailey called and said she'd be along to pick up her share in an hour or so."

"I can get them." Emily held out her hands from the top step, but Abel shook his head.

"You'd better let me. These buckets are kind of heavy."

He expected her to stick out that chin of hers and argue. For a second she looked like she was going to, but then she nodded back at him and smiled. "All right. Thanks." Emily reached over and pushed the screened door open wider for him. He had to pass right beside her to get on the porch.

She smelled good. Not perfumey, but fresh, like clean laundry mixed with some kind of girlie shampoo. He sidled past her, doing his best not to brush against her clothes because he knew his own smell at the moment was a lot less pleasant. He felt suddenly very aware of the sweat that darkened the armpits and back of his shirt and the dirt crusted on his arms and neck. His boots were leaving clumps of muck and mud all over the porch floor, too.

"Maybe I'd better just leave them here." He set the buckets down on the painted floorboards close to the door.

"That's fine." Emily didn't spare the brimming buckets a glance. She kept her eyes fastened on his face. "Listen, I hope you've worked up an appetite because I made a huge pecan coffee cake this morning, and I just took it out of the oven."

"Thanks, but I'd better be getting along home."

Emily's face fell. "Abel, we had a deal. You've kept on doing the chores after… Well, you've kept your end up, and I want to keep mine up. You haven't eaten a mouthful of my food for days, and if that keeps up, I'm going to have to assume our deal is off. Is it?"

She was looking at him intently, her gray-green eyes wide and worried. There were dustings of flour on her nose, and a tiny smear of batter on her left cheek. She had a faded rose-spattered apron of her grandmother's tied over her pink T-shirt, and her honey-gold hair was pulled up in a soft little roll on the back of her head.

She looked as heart-catchingly sweet as the first rosebud of the summer, and if he tried to sit across from her and eat right now, he'd choke on every bite.

"Well?" She lifted an eyebrow at him. "I know you've got that whole strong-and-silent thing going on, but I'd appreciate an answer. Do we have a deal or not?"

"I don't know." He hesitated and tried to think this through. As usual that was harder for him to do when Emily was within arm's length. She needed him to do the chores, and she was way too stubborn to let him do them for nothing. Both Emily and the animals would suffer if he couldn't get himself past this. Maybe she'd cracked his heart a little, but that wasn't really her fault. He'd been the one pushing things. And none of it changed the fact that he'd given her his word that he'd help her. "I'm pretty dirty today. I could take some of the cake with me, maybe."

Something flickered in her eyes. For a second Abel thought it was disappointment, but it was gone so fast that he couldn't be sure. She nodded. "That'll work, I guess. I'll wrap some up for you."

She went into the kitchen, and he took the opportunity to clean up a little at the utility sink angled in the corner of the shady porch. The cold well water coming through the old faucet felt good as he sluiced it over his face and the back of his neck. He cupped some of it in his hand and drank.

As he dried off with some paper towels, he breathed in the familiar odor of the porch, a mixture of paint, mint and old wood. It wasn't exactly a smell anybody would put in one of those air-freshener things, but it was a peaceful, homey scent.

The smell of the coffee cake that was wafting through the open kitchen doorway wasn't hurting things, either. Abel's empty stomach rumbled loudly just as Emily came back carrying a hefty chunk of cake in a plastic baggie.

"That's music to my ears," she said with a quick, cautious little smile. "Means you'll do justice to my cake."

"I always do," he replied, accepting the cake. Their fingers brushed briefly, and she jerked back as if he'd poked her with a stick. Something dark shuttered down over his heart. He gave her a brief nod.

"Thanks. I appreciate it. You have a good day, now. I'll be back over this evening," he said, and turned to go.

"Abel?"

He turned around. She was still standing on the porch, twisting her fingers in her apron and looking as twitchy as a jaybird balancing on a fence wire. He waited a second, but she just looked at him.

"Did you need me to do something else?"

Emily drew her lower lip into her mouth and nibbled. "Yes," she said finally. "Well, no. Actually I'm the one who needs to do something… I need to explain about the other day. About the horse, I mean."

Abel winced. "That's okay. You were in the right. I overstepped my bounds, and you set me straight, that's all. I've got no hard feelings if that's what's worrying you." He wished he had. Hard feelings would have been a sight easier to deal with than the ones he had flopping around inside him.

"Then why have you been avoiding me? And the twins—they've been so disappointed not to see you at suppertime. They've asked after you every single day. I didn't mean that we didn't want to see you at all, Abel. Truly I didn't. You've been a good friend to all of us, and we appreciate you. I'm really sorry if I made you think otherwise. I'm just…not looking for a relationship right now. That's all. But I really do value your friendship, and I don't want to lose that."

He shifted his weight from one muddy boot to the other, weighing the cake in his hand. He tried to think of something to say, some way to explain the knife twist he felt in his gut when he was around her and the twins now, but he came up empty. He couldn't even explain it to himself, much less to anybody else.

"Look," Emily said after an awkward few seconds, "I've got an hour and a half before I'm due at the coffee shop this morning, and the twins are already at the church day care. Why don't you come in? You can eat your cake with a nice cup of iced coffee, and we'll talk." He hesitated, and she reached across the space between them and put her hand on his forearm. "Please?"

He could feel every finger of her little hand on his arm, could feel that she was shaking just a little bit with nerves. This rift between them was worrying her, and as uncomfortable as he felt around her right now, he didn't like to think of Emily fretting. The protective wall he'd been building inside himself crumbled a little.

Abel sighed. He might as well face facts. This particular woman could ask him for pretty much anything, and if there was any way for him to get it for her, he would. It didn't make much sense, and given the way things stood, he was pretty sure it wasn't going to turn out all that well for him, but that was how it was.

"All right, then, if you're set on it. Some coffee'd be good." He didn't know what iced coffee was, but that didn't matter. He'd drink it.

The warm smile blooming on Emily's face halted when it was only half-formed and then turned into a frown as her eyes focused on something just past his right shoulder.

"Somebody's coming up the drive," she said, "and it's not Bailey. I can't think who it could be. I'm not expecting anybody else this morning. Cute car, though."

Abel turned to look. When he caught sight of the little car inching over the gravel, he felt like someone had just splashed him with ice water. Pine Valley was a small town, and there was only one person in it who drove a car like that one.

It had to be Jillian Marshall. Abel didn't know much about her except that she had hair the color of ripe red apples and a face full of freckles to match. If what he'd heard around town was true, her temper matched that flaming hair. Word was she wasn't a woman to be crossed if you could help it.

He also knew that her job had something to do with the foster care department of the local Family and Children's Services. That was the part that had him spooked.

Unless he missed his guess, there was a whole lot more than just a cute little car coming up Emily's driveway. That right there was big, scary trouble driving a bright purple Volkswagen Beetle.

Chapter Twelve

"Sit down and calm down, the both of you," Jillian Marshall said as she settled herself on the prim sofa in the Goosefeather Farm parlor and pulled a fat notebook and a ballpoint pen out of her purse. "Let's talk this out like rational people."

"Are you kidding me? You can't come out here and tell me somebody's started a child abuse investigation on me and expect me to stay *rational*." Emily was shaking like a leaf, but she couldn't sit down, couldn't stand still. She paced back and forth in front of the empty fireplace.

This was beyond horrible.

Jillian sighed. "I know. It stinks. But it's happened, and we have to deal with it. Rationally. So please sit down, Miss Elliott. Do you want Mr. Whitlock to stay?" Her sharp brown eyes cut over in his direction. "Is he an…um…interested party in this?" She looked back at Emily. "I'm going to have to ask you some pretty pointed questions, just so you know."

"I don't have anything to hide," Emily responded

through lips that had gone strangely numb. "From Abel or anybody else."

She felt Abel take her upper arm and guide her to her grandmother's old plush rocker. Gently but firmly he pushed her down into the chair. Then he quietly pulled up an embroidered footstool and sat down beside her, his long legs bent up so absurdly high that if the situation had been different, she'd have laughed.

There was nothing funny about what was happening here, though.

She probably should make Abel leave. She knew that her refusal to do so had given the caseworker the exact impression she'd been trying to squelch all over town, that she and Abel were in some kind of romantic relationship. At the moment, though, she couldn't have cared less. She needed Abel's comforting presence beside her. He was in his sock feet wearing a frayed shirt with some smears of garden soil on it, but his quiet strength was the only thing holding her together.

"All right." The social worker fixed them each with a stern eye. "First off, some ground rules. Nobody yells at me. Okay? I'm just the messenger here doing my job. Even when the circumstances of the complaint are a little suspicious, I am duty bound to complete a full investigation to make sure that the children are safe and well cared for."

"Who made the complaint?" Abel spoke up. There was something about the calm, deliberate way he asked his question that made Emily's spine straighten just a little. He meant business, and he was on her side. She wasn't alone in this. *Thank You, God.*

"Well, we often don't give out that information, but in this case, there's no reason I can't disclose the per-

son's identity. It'll come out anyway as the case pro-
ceeds. It's—"

"Lois Gordon," Emily finished with her. "You
should know that Mrs. Gordon and I have a history.
Her late son was my children's biological father. She
was never happy about Trey having a relationship with
me, and when I accidentally got pregnant, things got
worse. She blames me for the problems Trey had after I
left town, and she's upset that I'm back in Pine Valley."

"I appreciate the information, but it's not really relevant to my case, at least not at the moment. My only
job right now is to make sure that the kids aren't in any
danger." Jillian Marshall leaned back against the back
of the sofa, crossing one long leg over the other, ball-
point pen dangling idly from her fingers.

"What I'm trying to explain is that Lois Gordon has
a pretty big ax to grind where I'm concerned. I think
that's plenty relevant. She's not an unbiased reporter."

"I never thought she was." The social worker made a
couple of quick scrawls in her notebook. "I don't come
across that many unbiased reporters in my business.
Most people have an ax to grind if you dig down far
enough. I wish I could say that accounts like this were
usually generated by people with a genuine concern for
the children involved, but that actually happens a lot
less than you'd think. However, Mrs. Gordon's motivation for filing the report doesn't make a whole lot of
difference at this point. Once the complaint is made, I
have to follow through until I'm satisfied that there are
no grounds for further action."

"Emily's an excellent mother," Abel put in quickly.
"Miss Lois is wasting your time and the taxpayers'
money with this grudge of hers."

"Mrs. Gordon pays taxes, too, you know," the social worker responded mildly. "She's perfectly entitled to have her complaints heard. But as it happens, I'm inclined to agree with you. The workers at the church nursery had no concerns, and the children looked healthy and happy to me." She flipped back a couple of pages in her notebook. "No bruises, no suspicious injuries or scars of any kind, well nourished."

Emily flew out of her chair as if it were on fire. "*You went to the church nursery and talked to my children? Without my permission?*"

"No yelling, remember? Yes, of course I talked to your children. It's part of my job. Pastor Stone and the day care program director were both present, so everything was done exactly by the book. Don't worry. The kids are fine, and they have no idea about this investigation. And as I said, they showed no signs of neglect or abuse, and that works in your favor."

Abel came and stood beside Emily, and she felt the firm warmth of his hand on her arm. "Good. Then once Emily answers your questions, you can close this case and move on to one that actually has some truth to it."

Emily fastened her gaze hopefully on the social worker's face, but her heart dropped even before the other woman answered.

"It's not that simple. Don't get me wrong." The social worker held up her hands as both Abel and Emily started to speak. "I don't see any signs of abuse. That's true, but the allegations Mrs. Gordon is making go a little deeper than that. It's going to take time to sift through them thoroughly. And I'm going to have to be very thorough."

"Oh." Something in Jillian Marshall's voice tipped

Emily off. She looked intently at the redheaded woman sitting on her grandmother's couch. "I get it. Or at least I think I do."

The social worker shifted on the sofa, but she met Emily's gaze squarely. "Good. I hope you do. That'll make it easier for everybody."

"Am I missing something here?" Abel looked from one of the women to the other with his brow furrowed.

Emily responded without taking her eyes from Jillian Marshall's freckled face. "She'd close the case if it were up to her, but it isn't."

"Well, all right. If you're not in charge, who is?"

The social worker hesitated, and Emily answered for her. "Lois Gordon. Lois Gordon's the one calling the shots here, isn't she?"

There was a long pause. Emily was dimly aware that the goose was honking from the mint bed and that the grandfather clock in the hallway was ticking ponderously. She could see dust motes dancing in the shaft of sunlight that slanted through the parlor windows. She still hadn't gotten around to dusting in here.

None of it mattered. Time halted as Emily watched Jillian Marshall search for some way to balance truth and discretion in her reply.

"Mrs. Gordon is very well connected in Pine Valley. And yes, her allegations, no matter how far-fetched they may appear at face value, are unlikely to be dismissed by my supervisor without a very thorough investigation."

"Maybe I need to have a word with Mrs. Gordon," Abel suggested grimly.

"I really wouldn't advise that, Mr. Whitlock. In fact,

I would caution you both seriously against contacting Mrs. Gordon in any way. You'll only make things worse if you do." There was a brief pause before the social worker continued carefully. "However, I will suggest that you speak to a lawyer. Soon."

There was something about the precise way Jillian Marshall was choosing her words that chilled Emily to the bone. She couldn't speak. All she could do was stand on her grandmother's faded floral rug and stare at the woman across from her. The social worker suddenly found it hard to look Emily in the eye.

"Why does Emily need a lawyer? Mrs. Gordon may have powerful friends in Pine Valley, but they can't make truth out of lies. You've already seen the kids. You know they're all right, so your job is finished."

Jillian Marshall sighed. "Unfortunately for all of us in this room, I don't always get to decide when my job is finished. Not if I want to keep it."

"Please answer his question, Miss Marshall. Why do I need a lawyer?" Emily felt like she couldn't get quite enough air. The room felt too small.

The social worker rose to her feet, took a deep breath and met Emily's eyes. "You need to see a lawyer, Miss Elliott, because Lois Gordon isn't just making the allegation that you are an unfit mother. There's more to it than that."

Emily swallowed hard. "What else is there?"

"She's asking for guardianship of your children. In fact, she's petitioning for permanent custody. She wants to terminate your parental rights and adopt them. And honestly, given her level of clout around here, she's got a fighting chance at pulling it off."

* * *

Four hours later at his cabin, Abel put down his phone and scratched the last name off his list. That was it. He'd called everybody he knew who might have any influence in Pine Valley for advice and any help they might offer. It'd been a short list, and he'd gotten exactly nowhere.

The bleak picture Jillian Marshall had painted for them in Sadie Elliott's parlor was looking pretty accurate. Lois Gordon's late husband had been fishing buddies with the judge who'd be hearing this case, and since Dr. Gordon's death, Judge Callender was taking a particular interest in his friend's widow. All the people Abel had talked to had expressed the opinion that Emily had better lawyer up and fast. So the next thing he was going to do was find Emily the best attorney in the state of Georgia.

Lois Gordon wasn't taking the twins. Maybe he and Emily had things to work out, but this morning she'd leaned on him. She could have made him step outside, but instead she'd wanted him to stay. When he'd joined in the conversation, she'd let him.

Although Emily's independent streak was a mile wide and fathoms deep, this morning she'd turned to him, and that meant something. He wasn't sure exactly what it meant to Emily. Not yet. When all this dust had settled, he fully intended to find out.

But he already knew what it meant to him. It meant he'd move heaven and earth to make things come right for her. Lois Gordon was getting custody of Emily's twins over Abel Whitlock's dead body. That was all there was to it.

The first thing he needed to do was come up with

some money. He didn't know much about lawyers, but he knew they were expensive, and the better they were the more they cost. Emily didn't have any ready cash. Neither did he exactly, but he knew where he could get some.

Abel picked up his cell phone and punched in a number. He was just ending the call when he heard the knock.

Emily stood on his doorstep. Her face was pale, but there were some stubborn lines around her colorless mouth that encouraged him a little bit. They were both going to need every morsel of grit they could come up with.

"Emily, I was just about to call you. Come in and sit down. I've been thinking all this over, and I think the first thing we need to do—"

She cut him off. "I'm leaving, Abel. Today. Right now. I'm already packed up, and the twins are waiting in the car. I came over to tell you and to give you my key to the farmhouse." She held out the old-fashioned metal key.

"Emily." It was all he could say.

"My friend Clary knows a lawyer, and she asked for his advice. He said the best thing I could do in a situation like this was to relocate the case out of Pine Valley. If I'm residing in Atlanta, then the case will move there. So that's what I have to do. Lois Gordon's influence is local, and since there's no merit to the case, it should get resolved pretty fast. Hopefully."

"Listen to me, Emily." Abel's voice cracked with desperation, but he couldn't help it. He had an overwhelming urge to grab the beautiful, tired, frustrating woman in front of him and just never let go of her if that was what it would take to keep her from running away again. "Get the twins and come in. Let's talk this out before you decide what you're going to do."

"There's nothing else I *can* do, Abel. You know better than most people how Lois Gordon is, how this town works. Look at how your family's been talked about and treated around here over the years."

"My family deserved most of the stuff that was said about them, Emily. You're not in the wrong here. That's the difference. This will come right in the end. You'll see. You just need to have a little faith."

"I can't risk losing my children," Emily argued shakily. She cleared her throat and took a careful breath. "I *won't* risk it. Nothing's worth that, certainly not a stupid old farm." Her voice broke as she forced out the words, and in spite of the mess they were in, Abel's heart lifted a fraction.

That hitch in her voice told him Emily didn't think Goosefeather Farm was just a stupid old place, not anymore. She was actually sorry to leave it, and that was what he'd been hoping for all along.

Well, it was part of what he'd been hoping for.

"Look, I know this has you running scared, but we can figure it out. I've been making some phone calls. First off, we'll need a really good lawyer. I know money's an issue, but I can help with that."

Emily's expression didn't soften. "I appreciate that, Abel. I really do, but I'm sticking to my plan."

She wasn't listening to him. He bit back his frustration and tried to speak evenly. "You don't have to handle this on your own, Emily. You've got to let me help you."

"There's nothing you can do. I've already heard from a good lawyer, and I'm taking his advice. The twins and I will move back in with Clary, and Mr. Alvarez has agreed to give me my job back. I'll be all right. As long as I have Paul and Phoebe, I'll be fine." She tilted her pale chin up in that gesture that always pinched his heart.

She took his hand in hers and pressed the cool metal key into his palm. "Goosefeather Farm is all yours, Abel, or it will be as soon as Mr. Monroe hears I've left. Knowing that you're the one who's going to have it makes leaving a little easier. It really should have been yours to start with. I see that now. You're the one who loves all those crazy animals. You're the one who knows how to take care of the fields and the equipment and everything that goes with that place. Grandma should have just left it to you outright. I wish she had." Emily gave him a watery smile. "I sure could have done without this whole mess."

"I don't want Goosefeather Farm, Emily. Not this way, not without you there, not without the twins." Abel dropped the key onto the planks of his cabin floor, where it clanged once and went silent. He took both of Emily's hands in his and looked into her face. He prayed hard for the right words, because without God's help he knew he would never be able to say it the right way, the best way.

"Listen to me, Emily. This whole mess you're talking about? It may have been one to you, but it's been the best time I've ever had. I've never had a family to speak of, and I didn't really know what I was missing until you and the twins came along. Now that I do, I can't even look at life without you. I know I'm probably saying this all wrong, doing this all wrong. But I can't help that. I reckon I've got to say it, and you've got to hear it. I love you. And Paul. And Phoebe. I love all of you."

"Abel." Emily was crying. "Don't do this. Please. Just don't."

"I have to." He took a tighter grip on her hands and leaned down, trying to hold her eyes with his own. "I'm over my head in love with you. I know I'm not the kind of man you had in mind, and I can't offer you the life you've got all picked out for yourself. I'm not bringing much to this table except a family name that won't do us any favors around here. I know that. But you know *me*, Emily, and what I am...*all* I am belongs to you and the twins. Surely that ought to count for something. We can figure the rest of it out together. Look, I know trusting doesn't come easily to you. I know why, and I've tried to be patient, but now we're out of time. So I'm asking you to stay here and trust me. And I promise you." He tilted her chin up so she had to meet his eyes. "I *promise* you, Emily, I won't let you down."

For a second, those wide tear-soaked gray-green eyes looked into his, and he thought somehow he'd managed to get through all those walls she'd built around herself, that he'd broken through her defenses and into that well-guarded heart of hers.

Then she shook her head. "I can't, Abel. I'm sorry. I just can't." Quickly she released herself from his grip and fled down the wooden steps of his porch. Minutes later her little car slipped out of sight down his winding driveway, and she was gone.

Chapter Thirteen

A month later Emily stood in her apartment's cramped living room and eyed the large box on the coffee table. Abel's name was scrawled on the return address label, and the sticky note Clary had added said *Delivered this afternoon.*

Emily untied her green-striped Café Cup apron with shaking fingers. She really didn't need this, not now. She couldn't look back. She had to stay focused on how well things were working out for her here in Atlanta.

The lawyer had gotten the custody case dismissed, something that would never have happened in Pine Valley, not with Lois Gordon pulling every string she could get her hands on.

Emily still had her job, and Mr. Alvarez seemed more appreciative now that he'd done without her for a while. He was even hinting about promoting her to assistant manager, which would mean a small pay raise and more regular hours.

And the twins had happily gone off to their very first sleepover party this evening, so hopefully the hardest part of this abrupt transition back to city life was finally behind them.

It all proved that she'd made the right decision, and she didn't need some box bringing up the memory of Abel's face when she'd left him standing beside that lonesome chair on his front porch.

Well, the porch that stretched across the front of Grandma's farmhouse held two rocking chairs. One day he'd find the right woman for the second one, someone who milked cows from the right side and who never picked butter beans before they were ready, and who was happy to let his big shoulders carry her burdens.

The box blurred, and Emily blinked hard. She was so *tired* of crying, and it was pointless anyway. Maybe her feelings for Abel had been deeper than she'd realized, but what was done was done. That look on Abel's face…there was just no going back from that.

"Please, Lord," she prayed, "heal whatever hurt I caused him. Bring him joy, because he's a good man, and he deserves it. And please help me because I've got to open this box, and I have a feeling whatever's in here is just going to make me feel worse. And honestly I don't think I can take it."

She swallowed hard, slit the packing tape and opened the cardboard flaps.

The inside was crammed with wads of brown paper. She unwrapped one and a delicately carved chess knight rolled onto her palm.

She unwrapped piece after piece and set them on the table. When the chess set was completed, Goosefeather Farm's animals started to appear: Beulah the cow, Newman the rooster, Cherry the goat and her twin kids and finally Glory, wings outstretched, looking for all the world as if she were about to honk.

A tear splattered on Glory's head, and Emily wiped it away with her thumb. She actually missed that crazy goose. She missed so many things about Goosefeather Farm: the peace, the fresh scent of the air, her work at the coffee shop, the comforting warmth of the old-fashioned kitchen…

But mostly she missed Abel.

The last paper ball unveiled a slim twig adorned with a bloom of dogwood. The piece was exquisitely carved and so delicate that she didn't know how it had survived its journey intact. She turned it over, and her heart caught.

Emily was carved in script on the bottom.

Abel must have spent hours on this, thinking of her as he formed each petal, and after the way she'd hurt him, it was no wonder he hadn't wanted to keep it.

She set the blossom gently aside. In the bottom of the box was a heavy square shrouded in more paper. She ripped it away, revealing a checkerboard pattern. It was Paul's chessboard and taped to it was an envelope bearing her name.

She pulled it free, tracing the scrawl of Abel's handwriting with a trembling finger. Emily fought a silly impulse to lift the envelope to her nose and see if it held his scent, that tangy mix of pine needles and wood shavings and sun-warmed hay.

That smell was another thing she missed.

The envelope contained only a rectangle of blue official-looking paper. Emily unfolded it and gasped, her heart plummeting.

What had Abel done?

* * *

Abel set down his chisel and eyed the half-finished piece on his workbench with a sinking feeling. He considered it from a couple of angles before he gave up, unclamped it and tossed it into the overflowing box of abandoned projects.

He opened the little refrigerator humming under the window and grabbed a bottle of water. Dropping into a handy chair, he closed his eyes and drank.

He had to get past this. Emily and the twins were already out of his life. He couldn't lose his carving, too.

He heard the car crunching up his driveway, but he kept his eyes closed and stayed put. He didn't know who it was, and he didn't care. He meant to install a gate at the bottom of his driveway before the week was out. He might as well work on that, since he couldn't do anything else.

There was a sudden banging on the door. The doorknob rattled, and a female voice demanded, "Abel Whitlock, you let me in!"

Emily.

The knob rattled again. "Open this door! We need to talk."

Abel set the water bottle on top of the fridge, rose and moved toward the door. Everything felt like it was unfolding in slow motion as his brain struggled to catch up.

Emily was back. Not only that, but for some reason she was pitching a fit that was probably blistering the paint right off his door.

He slid the dead bolt aside with clumsy fingers. Emily stood on his step dappled with moonlight, fists on her hips.

The sight of her struck him like a baseball bat to the stomach. She had her hair scraped into a high ponytail, but the curly bits had pulled loose and were framing her face like they always did. If she was wearing any makeup, he couldn't tell it, and she had on a dark green golf shirt with *Café Cup* and a steaming coffee cup logo embroidered over her heart. She looked so beautiful he couldn't breathe.

She also looked mad enough to bite a chunk out of him.

"What's this?" She waved a little blue rectangle in front of his nose, and he managed to look away from her face long enough to identify it.

"It's a check."

"You know what I mean! Where'd you get this money, Abel?"

So she was here to fuss about the check. Abel's heart turned to stone and sank to the pit of his stomach. "I don't see how that's any of your business, Emily."

"See right there?" Emily jabbed a finger at the top line of the check. "That's my name, and that makes it my business! Tell me." She swallowed hard. "Did you sell the farm?"

"What difference does it make to you if I did?"

Her face crumpled. "I never asked you to sell the farm. I never *wanted* you to sell it! I told you I could handle my problems by myself, and I did. The custody case is settled. We didn't even have to go to court."

"I heard." He walked over and retrieved his water bottle even though he wasn't thirsty anymore, wasn't anything anymore.

"You heard. Then why…?" Emily indicated the check in her hand.

"That money's yours." He dropped back into his chair and took a swallow of his water, although his stomach was churning so hard he wasn't sure it would stay down.

Yeah, he should throw up. That would help.

"I don't want it."

"Sure you do." Abel blew out a tired breath. "Relax. There are no strings attached."

"I'm not taking this money, Abel." She set the check on the table next to him. "Maybe it's not too late for you to get the farm back. I know you had your heart set on keeping it."

He couldn't take much more of this. He lifted his head and looked her straight in her greenish eyes. "Goosefeather Farm isn't what I had my heart set on keeping, Emily. I think I made that pretty clear."

She flushed, and her eyes swam with tears.

"I'm so sorry," she whispered.

"Don't be. You did what you felt like you had to do. And it sounds like you were right. It all worked out."

"Not for you." She reached over and put her hand on his arm.

He winced. "Don't make this worse than it already is."

"I know I didn't...listen to you that day. It's just..." Her voice wavered. "It wasn't the first time a man told me he loved me and made me all kinds of promises, you know?" A tear streaked down her face, and she made an irritated noise and swiped it away. "I am *not* going to cry. I'm just not. I was terrified that Lois was going to take the twins, Abel. I had to make sure that couldn't happen. Can't you understand?"

"Sure. I understand. You were scared. So you ran

away to handle it by yourself because that's what you do. You handle things by yourself." He rubbed his hand over his brow. Might as well get this over with. "It took me a while, but now I get it. There's no room in your life for a man like me, Emily."

Emily's eyebrows drew together, and her chin tilted up a fraction. "What do you mean, *a man like you*? Abel, you can't honestly believe this has anything to do with your family! Because it doesn't!"

"No, you're right. This isn't about who my father was or who my grandfather was. It's about who I am, and that's where we hit a snag. You don't want a man like me, Emily. I just can't let the woman I love handle trouble and hard work by herself even if that's the way she wants it. I'm not made that way." He met her eyes squarely. "I'm not Trey Gordon."

"I know that!" She sounded defensive.

"I don't think you do. I think you've been sizing me up by his measure ever since you came back to Pine Valley, and I'm right tired of it. You ought to know by now that I've got nothing in common with the likes of a man who'd turn his back on the girl carrying his babies. Do you honestly think for one minute that if those twins were mine I'd have left you to shoulder that alone? Do you think I'd have let my *mother* or anybody else for that matter stand between me and you?"

"No, but I didn't think Trey would, either. I guess I'm a pretty poor judge of character." Emily's chin was still up, but it was trembling. "I truly never wanted things to turn out like this."

His anger dissolved abruptly into the tired sadness that had been plaguing him since she left. This was going nowhere. "It's probably for the best. You've got your future all planned out, and I know those plans mean a lot to you. They make you feel safe, safer than I can, I guess. I want you to feel safe, Emily, you and the twins. If marrying me won't do it, maybe the money will." He pushed the check closer to her with his finger. "Take it. I won't feel right about things if you don't."

There was a second of silence. When he looked up he saw that Emily's face had gone paper white, and her eyes were wide.

"What?" he asked her irritably.

Her neck pulsed as she swallowed. "Marrying you?"

She seemed genuinely surprised, and Abel shook his head. "I'm not a complicated man, Emily. When I tell a woman I love her, marrying her goes with that territory."

"I think... I think I need to sit down." Her voice sounded strangely thin. Abel took one hard look at her face and moved fast. Five seconds later he had her in a chair with her head down between her knees, breathing into a brown paper sack he'd yanked from his trash can.

"Are you all right?" Abel's voice seemed to come from miles above her. Emily kept her eyes closed and breathed deep.

"This bag smells like chocolate," she said.

"I've been missing your cooking," he said. She could hear a thread of amusement in his voice.

This wasn't amusing. This was embarrassing.

Slowly Emily straightened back up in her chair. She wadded the paper sack and tossed it in the trash before raising her eyes to meet Abel's.

There were tired lines around his mouth, but his eyes

held a faint twinkle…and a glimmer of something else behind that.

It was the something else she spoke to. "You," she repeated, keeping her eyes locked on his, "never said anything to me about marriage."

He didn't blink. "I know I'm not great with words, but it seems to me I made things plain enough. Like I said, if you don't know what 'I love you' means when it comes from somebody like me, then you don't understand what kind of man I am, Emily." His eyes stayed steady on hers.

Steady.

He was wrong. She'd been wrong before, but he was wrong now. She knew exactly what kind of man Abel Whitlock was.

He was steady.

"You sent the chess set and the animals to the twins," she said suddenly.

Now he blinked. Then nodded. "I did. I promised them those things."

And this man kept his promises, even the little ones.

"And the dogwood was for me. It had my name on it."

"I made it for you. It was yours."

"Then there was that ridiculous check."

Something steely flickered into his gaze. "I told you I didn't want your inheritance, Emily. I meant it. That money belongs to you."

"Harder to move than a sack of bees," she quoted softly.

"What?"

"So, that's the deal? I can take either you or the money for the farm?"

The hope that leaped into his eyes warmed her heart. "That's about the size of it, I reckon."

A pause stretched between them, pregnant with possibilities. Emily studied the man in front of her. He still looked the tiniest bit exasperated, but the lines in his face spoke of patience and endurance, and the set of his shoulders meant strength.

When this man spoke of love, it was tied so hard in his heart to commitment that he didn't even think it was necessary to mention it.

That was the kind of man he was.

"Somebody once told me that if a decent man wants something, he asks for it straight out." Emily lifted an eyebrow. "Maybe you should give that a shot."

The sideways smile she loved lit up his lean face.

"All right," he said. "If that's what you want, I'll say it straight out. Emily, I love you so much my life falls to bits without you. I'll tell you up front I'm not much of a prize. I'm probably going to mess up every one of those pretty plans you're so fond of and drive you crazy because I've never loved anybody like I love you, and I don't have a clue how to do it. And you'd better take a real good look at what you're getting because I don't change easy. I never have, and I most likely never will. If I were a piece of wood, I'd be a chunk of oak with a stubborn grain that you can hardly get a chisel in. But I'll last, Emily. I'll last, and I'll love you and those twins until the last day the sun rises for me. You have my word on that."

"You still haven't asked me anything," she chided softly. She stood and closed the gap between them. His woodsy scent enveloped her, and it felt like coming home.

"Do I actually have to ask?" There was a pained twinkle in his eye now. "With words?"

"I think that's generally how it's done."

"All right, then." He took a deep breath. "Will you marry me, Emily?"

She smiled. "Absolutely. Yes. This minute, if you want me to."

His blue eyes held hers, and the corner of his mouth quirked. "You know, that worked out mighty well. Maybe I'm better at this talking thing than I thought."

"Don't you count on it. Those five words probably just got you into the most trouble of any you've ever said, because you're stuck with me now, Abel Whitlock. You'd better take a good look at what you're getting, too. I stink at farming, and I'm used to doing things my own way, and I come complete with twins, who are going to be so happy to see you again that they'll never give you a minute's peace. The three of us are going to try that legendary patience of yours right to its limits. And when that happens, please just remember that I think you're the kindest, strongest, *finest* man I've ever met and that I love you beyond all reason. And," she added mischievously, "that you asked for it."

There was a suspicious shimmer in his eyes, and he shook his head. "Now I really don't know what to say."

"Now I think words are optional." She tiptoed and pressed her lips to his crooked mouth.

He took charge of the kiss easily, and when he finally lifted his lips from hers, she sank back into the chair.

It was another weak-kneed girlie moment for Emily Elliott.

She'd probably better get used to those.

He knelt in front of her, giving her the unusual experience of looking straight into the tall man's eyes as he gathered both her hands in his. "Before we start making any more plans, Emily, there's something I've got to tell you."

Her heart fluttered, but she shook her head resolutely. "Whatever it is, it doesn't matter. I trust you."

"Well, now, it might matter. Just a little."

His eyes were twinkling. Surely that meant it couldn't be bad news. "All right." Emily braced herself. "What is it?"

"I didn't sell the farm. It's still mine. Ours, as it turns out."

"You didn't sell? Oh, Abel, I'm so glad!" Emily frowned. "But if you didn't sell Goosefeather Farm, where'd that money come from?"

"I sold the buck."

"What?" Emily whirled and saw the pedestal standing empty in its corner. "Oh, no! That carving meant so much to you!" She felt her tears starting again.

"You and the twins mean more," he answered simply. "No, now, don't cry over it. That buck already served his purpose. Now that I've got you, Emily, I sure won't need any other reminders of how much God has blessed me."

"But if you didn't sell Goosefeather, where'd the rest of the money come from? Surely you didn't get all that from selling one carving?"

"Most of it." Abel shrugged. "Somebody'd been hankering after that buck for a while, but I was stubborn about selling it. He'd have given me more if I'd asked." He smiled. "The truth is, I've been selling my carvings for a while now, and folks seem to like them well enough to pay steep prices for the better ones. I'm no millionaire, but I figure I can take care of you and the twins just fine, along with any other babies we might have."

Babies. And not just any babies. Abel's babies with his dark hair and blue eyes. Emily's heart lurched, and she clamped down on his big hand as if her life depended on it.

"Abel?"

"What is it, darlin'?"

"I think… I think I'm going to need that paper bag again."

Epilogue

"I'm so sorry," Clary said breathlessly. "I had the ring tied to the bouquet ribbon for safekeeping." Emily's maid of honor brandished her nosegay of creamy roses as evidence. "That goose took it right off."

"Glory was just jealous. She's happy now because she's got everybody's attention." Emily watched through her veil as Clary discarded her heels and hitched up her yellow dress. She, Bailey and Pastor Stone, the tails of his gray suit flapping behind him, chased Glory through the white folding chairs arranged between the blooming plum trees. The twins, who'd looked so pristine and perfect in their wedding attire just a few minutes ago, ran after them shrieking.

Lois Gordon in her prim lavender suit hobbled behind them as fast as her heels allowed. "Phoebe, Paul! Come to Nana, darlings! You'll spoil your clothes!"

Emily started to step out of her spot to corral her children, but Abel caught her gently by the arm.

"Let Lois handle it," he murmured. He smiled, and the combination of his particular smile and the gray suit he was wearing knocked every other thought out of Emily's head.

Oh, how she loved this man!

She smiled back at him. "They really will ruin their outfits."

"Oh, now, I don't know about that. Miss Lois seems pretty determined." They watched together as Lois cleared a shrub in pursuit of her grandchildren. "And she's spry for her age."

"You were right about letting her spend time with the twins," Emily admitted. "She's turning out to be a pretty stellar grandmother."

"Forgiveness is generally the best thing all around," Abel said quietly. "Watch and see. Those twins will make all the difference to that woman. Love's the surest cure for grief there is."

The flapping goose and her pursuers looped back by, and Emily shook her head ruefully. "At least Glory's not honking, so hopefully she's still got the ring in her beak. She'd better have. If she's swallowed your wedding ring, Abel, I'm cooking that bird for Sunday dinner. I mean it!"

Jacob Stone took a flying leap at the goose, who had her wings outstretched and was running for all she was worth. He missed and went down in a spectacular belly flop, which startled Glory enough that she flew right up into Bailey's face. The disheveled bridesmaid snagged the struggling bird in midair.

"Gotcha!" A second later she held up the ring, and the wedding guests cheered.

The bridesmaids rejoined the wedding party, and Bailey handed the ring over to Emily with a flash of her perfect smile. "Crisis averted!" Bailey slid into place beside Clary, brushing away Emily's whispered apology with another grin. "Are you kidding me? This is hands down the most fun I've ever had at a wedding!"

Glory ducked into the pasture where a heavily pregnant Beulah was quietly cropping grass and ignoring the entire spectacle. The goose sidled close to the cow for safety, then let out a series of loud honks as Pastor Stone, breathing hard, resumed his position under the flower-decked trellis.

Lois, beaming triumphantly, shepherded the twins carefully back into position. She tweaked the hem of Phoebe's creamy dress into place and darted a tentative smile up at Emily before sinking back in her seat, eyes fastened on her giggling grandchildren.

"Now," Jacob Stone muttered, "where were we?" He leaned over and retrieved a leather binder from the grass. He flipped it open, throwing a baleful look toward the protesting goose. "I think we've pretty well covered the 'if anybody objects' part."

"You're burning daylight, Stone." Abel looked deep into Emily's eyes and smiled his crooked smile. "Get to it."

"Don't rush me, Whitlock. Some things take time if you're going to do them right." Stone paged through his book. "I *think* we were halfway through the rings."

"Fine. Start there and let's get this finished. I'd like this pretty lady married to me before she changes her mind."

"Any chance of you changing your mind, Emily?" The minister raised a questioning eyebrow.

"Nope." Emily smiled at her groom and tilted up her chin. "No chance at all." Without waiting for her prompt, she slipped the rescued ring on Abel's finger.

His twinkling eyes grew serious as he folded her veil carefully back over her hair, his roughened hands snagging slightly on the delicate threads.

The minister nodded. "Good enough. Then by the authority vested in me by the state of Georgia, I now pronounce you husband and wife. Finally. Now hurry up and kiss your bride, Whitlock," he added, "before that goose honks herself inside out."

"Don't rush me, Stone." Abel held Emily's eyes as he leaned toward her, the smile she loved quirking up the corner of his mouth. "Some things take time if you're going to do them right."

* * * * *

If you enjoyed A FAMILY FOR THE FARMER,
look for these other emotionally gripping
and wonderful stories

THE RANCHER'S TEXAS MATCH by Brenda Minton
LONE STAR DAD by Linda Goodnight
FALLING FOR THE SINGLE DAD by Lisa Carter

Available now from Love Inspired!

Find more great reads at www.LoveInspired.com.

Dear Reader,

Come on in! I'll put some fresh apple muffins on a plate, pour you a nice glass of sweet iced tea and we'll settle in for a visit here at the scrubbed kitchen table of Goosefeather Farm.

There's just something about a farm, isn't there? A farm can serve as an oasis of peace and old-fashioned values in the middle of a rushed and confusing world. It's a place for family, for deep and abiding friendships and sometimes, as we saw with Abel and Emily, even for falling in love! Of course, as little Phoebe pointed out, there's also plenty of hard work and dirt, but in the end it's all worth it!

I admit I might be just a tiny bit biased—my family and I live on a Georgia farm very similar to Goosefeather, and we love it! In fact, I "borrowed" several of our own quirky animals for this story! Beulah the milk cow, Glory the goose and Cherry the goat greet me every single morning, and I wouldn't have it any other way!

Thanks so much for visiting with me on Goosefeather Farm, and feel free to come back anytime! The back door's never locked, you're always welcome and I have a feeling that this old place has lots more sweet stories to tell us. In the meantime, if you want to chat, drop me a line at laurelblountwrites@gmail.com. I'd love to hear from you!

Laurel Blount

COMING NEXT MONTH FROM

Love Inspired®

Available October 18, 2016

THE RANGER'S TEXAS PROPOSAL
Lone Star Cowboy League: Boys Ranch
by Jessica Keller

When Texas Ranger Heath Grayson finds pregnant widow Josie Markham working her ranch alone, he insists on helping. Josie's vowed never to fall for a lawman again, but she soon realizes he could be the final piece to her growing family.

AMISH CHRISTMAS BLESSINGS
by Marta Perry and Jo Ann Brown

In these two brand-new novellas, Christmas reunites one Amish beauty with a past love, while another will be led headfirst into her future by a handsome Amish farmer.

THE COWBOY'S CHRISTMAS BABY
Big Sky Cowboys • by Carolyne Aarsen

Former rodeo star Dean Moore is eager to find a new path after an accident cut his career short. Reuniting with former crush and single mom Erin McCauley to fix up her home in time for the holidays could be his second chance with the one who got away.

THE PASTOR'S CHRISTMAS COURTSHIP
Hearts of Hunter Ridge • by Glynna Kaye

Retreating to her grandparents' mountain cabin for Christmas, city girl Jodi Thorpe is looking to rebuild after a tragic loss. She never expects to be roped into a charity project—or that the pastor running the program is the former bad-boy crush she's never forgotten.

A MOM FOR CHRISTMAS
Home to Dover • by Lorraine Beatty

As she heals from an injury, ballerina Bethany Montgomery agrees to put on her hometown's Christmas extravaganza before heading back to her career. But when she discovers old love—and single dad—Noah Carlisle, is also back in town, can she make room for a new dream: becoming a wife and mom?

HIS HOLIDAY MATCHMAKER
Texas Sweethearts • by Kat Brookes

All little Katie Cooper wants for Christmas is a mommy. But Nathan Cooper isn't prepared for his daughter's matchmaking—or to find himself under the mistletoe with interior designer Alyssa McCall as they work on the town's new recreation center.

LOOK FOR THESE AND OTHER LOVE INSPIRED BOOKS WHEREVER BOOKS ARE SOLD, INCLUDING MOST BOOKSTORES, SUPERMARKETS, DISCOUNT STORES AND DRUGSTORES.

LICNM1016

REQUEST YOUR FREE BOOKS!

2 FREE INSPIRATIONAL NOVELS
PLUS 2
FREE
MYSTERY GIFTS

Love Inspired®

YES! Please send me 2 FREE Love Inspired® novels and my 2 FREE mystery gifts (gifts are worth about $10). After receiving them, if I don't wish to receive any more books, I can return the shipping statement marked "cancel." If I don't cancel, I will receive 6 brand-new novels every month and be billed just $4.99 per book in the U.S. or $5.49 per book in Canada. That's a saving of at least 17% off the cover price. It's quite a bargain! Shipping and handling is just 50¢ per book in the U.S. and 75¢ per book in Canada.* I understand that accepting the 2 free books and gifts places me under no obligation to buy anything. I can always return a shipment and cancel at any time. Even if I never buy another book, the two free books and gifts are mine to keep forever.   105/305 IDN GH5P

Name   (PLEASE PRINT)

Address   Apt. #

City   State/Prov.   Zip/Postal Code

Signature (if under 18, a parent or guardian must sign)

Mail to the **Reader Service:**
IN U.S.A.: P.O. Box 1867, Buffalo, NY 14240-1867
IN CANADA: P.O. Box 609, Fort Erie, Ontario L2A 5X3

Are you a subscriber to Love Inspired® books and want to receive the larger-print edition?
Call 1-800-873-8635 or visit www.ReaderService.com.

* Terms and prices subject to change without notice. Prices do not include applicable taxes. Sales tax applicable in N.Y. Canadian residents will be charged applicable taxes. Offer not valid in Quebec. This offer is limited to one order per household. Not valid for current subscribers to Love Inspired books. All orders subject to credit approval. Credit or debit balances in a customer's account(s) may be offset by any other outstanding balance owed by or to the customer. Please allow 4 to 6 weeks for delivery. Offer available while quantities last.

Your Privacy—The Reader Service is committed to protecting your privacy. Our Privacy Policy is available online at www.ReaderService.com or upon request from the Reader Service.

We make a portion of our mailing list available to reputable third parties that offer products we believe may interest you. If you prefer that we not exchange your name with third parties, or if you wish to clarify or modify your communication preferences, please visit us at www.ReaderService.com/consumerchoice or write to us at Reader Service Preference Service, P.O. Box 9062, Buffalo, NY 14240-9062. Include your complete name and address.

LII5

What happens when a Texas Ranger determined to stay single meets a pregnant widow who unwittingly works her way into his heart?

Read on for a sneak preview of the second book in the
LONE STAR COWBOY LEAGUE: BOYS RANCH
miniseries, THE RANGER'S TEXAS PROPOSAL
by Jessica Keller.

"What can I do for you, Officer?" Josie Markham's tone said she didn't really want to do anything for him. Ever.

He raised his eyebrows.

"White hat. Boots. White starched shirt. And that belt's the type they only issue to Texas Rangers." She gestured toward his holster. "I hope you weren't trying to be undercover."

"Good eye." He extended his hand. She narrowed her gaze but shook it. "Heath Grayson. I'm a friend of Flint's."

In the space of a heartbeat, her hesitant expression vanished and was replaced by wide-eyed concern. "Did something else happen at the boys ranch?" She shifted from around the wheelbarrow. "What are we waiting for? If something's wrong, let's go."

Once she moved away from the wheelbarrow, he saw her stomach. Pregnant. Very pregnant. Flint had mentioned Josie was widowed, but he'd left out the little detail that she was with child. So a recent widow.

Had she been in the barn alone…doing chores?

"Let me help you with your chores," Heath said.

Josie's jaw dropped. "What about the boys ranch?"

"The ranch is fine."

"Why didn't you say so? You about gave me a heart attack." She laid her hand on her chest and took a few deep breaths. Then her eyes skirted back up to capture his. "If the ranch is fine, why exactly are you here then?"

She fanned her face and dragged in huge amounts of oxygen through her mouth as if she was having a hard time getting it into her lungs.

Now he'd done it. Gone and gotten a pregnant woman all worked up. Did he need to find her a chair? A drink of water? Rush her to the hospital? What a terrible feeling, being out of control. It was disconcerting.

"Are you all right, ma'am? What do you need?"

"I'm fine. Just fine." She laughed. "You should see your face, though." She pointed up at him and covered her mouth, hiding her wide grin. Her warm brown eyes shone with mischief. "Now you look like you're the one having a heart attack. Relax there, Officer. It was only a figure of speech." Her laugh was a high sound, full of joy. Josie laughed with her whole self, without holding anything back.

Heath wanted to hear it again.

Don't miss
THE RANGER'S TEXAS PROPOSAL
by Jessica Keller, available November 2016 wherever
Love Inspired® books and ebooks are sold.

www.LoveInspired.com

LIEXP1016

Love the Love Inspired
book you just read?

Your opinion matters.

**Review this book on your favorite
book site, review site, blog or your own
social media properties and share your
opinion with other readers!**